THE TORIES

Mudlark
HarperCollins*Publishers*
1 London Bridge Street
London SE1 9GF

www.harpercollins.co.uk

HarperCollins*Publishers*
Macken House, 39/40 Mayor Street Upper
Dublin 1, D01 C9W8, Ireland

First published by Mudlark 2024

1 3 5 7 9 10 8 6 4 2

© Henry Morris 2024

Henry Morris asserts the moral right to
be identified as the author of this work

A catalogue record of this book is
available from the British Library

ISBN 978-0-00-870900-6

Printed and bound in the UK using 100% renewable
electricity at CPI Group (UK) Ltd

All rights reserved. No part of this publication may be
reproduced, stored in a retrieval system, or transmitted,
in any form or by any means, electronic, mechanical,
photocopying, recording or otherwise, without the prior
written permission of the publishers.

MIX
Paper | Supporting
responsible forestry
FSC
www.fsc.org   FSC™ C007454

This book is produced from independently certified FSC™
paper to ensure responsible forest management.

For more information visit: www.harpercollins.co.uk/green

THE MOST TROUBLESOME RAIGNE AND MOST LAMENTABLE TRAGEDIE OF THE TORIES

With the most tragicall falls of proud Cameron, May, Johnson, Truss and Sunak

As it was sundrie times publiquely acted in the honourable citie of London, by the honourable the Earle of Pembroke his servants.

MUDLARK

INTRODUCTION

A BRIEF VIEW OF THE PLAY

The Most Troublesome Raigne and Most Lamentable Tragedie of the Tories, with its persistent catastrophes and failures, penetrating exploration of greed and incompetence, and relentlessly self-referential style, is a play like no other. It stands apart from the rest of the Shakespeare output as his only self-satirising tragicomedy, and one that speaks directly to the twenty-first century.

Along with *Cardenio* and *Love's Labour's Won*, *The Tragedie* was presumed lost to time, until a battered quarto fell out of the back of a copy of *How Green Was My Valley* in a bookshop in Aberteifi, west Wales, in 1939. The fact that this isn't the most interesting thing about the play is testament to its significance.

While *The Tragedie of the Tories* is firmly rooted in Jacobean culture, it seems to have held a prophetic hand to the fevered forehead of the future.

Academic consensus tells us that the play was likely written at the end of 1607, marking the culmination of Shakespeare's gilded era, and leading us into his late romances. However, there is some divergence of opinion, with scholars at both MIT and Lampeter arguing that in the Act V Scene 5 discovery of Cameron by Sunak in his Shepherd's Hut, Shakespeare was not anticipating *The Winter's Tale*, but echoing it. This would then move the date to 1611.

Henry Morris, the editor who has studied *The Tragedie* more closely than any other, approaches the text through its most important contexts: theatricality, the language and its unflinching exploration of the venal. 'It almost goes without saying that the most remarkable thing about this play is Shakespeare's willingness to borrow from himself.'

If anyone else did this it would be called plagiarising, but because Shakespeare is mugging himself, it is fine. Kenneth Tynan famously described it as 'a best of that which wouldn't be out of place in the Channel 5 Christmas schedules', while, upon the formation of David Cameron's first government in 2010, Charlotte Rampling called it an 'astonishingly prescient vision of the exact chronology of early twenty-first-century UK politics'.

The narrative follows the Tories' descent from their alleged heights of Bullingdon Conservativism – that aggregation of Etonian-educated parasites presumed born to rule – to the depths of Red Wall nativism in which verse and earthy, comic prose are deployed with such agility you could be forgiven for thinking you are in the hands of a high D, possibly low C grade A-level student.

The Tragedie was Laurence Olivier's least favourite play. With its five anti-heroes and a seemingly inexhaustible cast of grotesques, Olivier wryly referred to it as 'attritional' and wondered 'how many penny groundlings made it to the interval'. According to Melvyn Bragg, on the other hand, the play is more helpfully approached as a proto-Brechtian enigma. 'By placing no likeable characters on the stage at any point, Shakespeare invites the audience to do something I haven't seen happen since *Triangle*: to root for themselves.'

Much has been written about prophecy and the protagonists' names. Cameron, May, Johnson, Truss and Sunak are all future rulers of the United Kingdom. This external analogue of the Widdecombes' prediction of future rulers inside the play raises the tantalising question: was Shakespeare supernaturally gifted? Or is the answer more prosaic; might this extraordinary coincidence be explained by laws of probability? It is said that a monkey hitting a typewriter at random for an infinite amount of time will eventually produce the works of Shakespeare. So, statistically, should it be surprising that letting a mind as big as Shakespeare's loose on his own ideas might result in him producing the *Complete Works of Shakespeare*?*

In which case, we should raise our eyebrows no higher than those of Bernard Ingham to accept that Shakespeare not only anticipated the names, but also the subterfuges, ploys, tricks and betrayals of these political characters. Human weakness, as manifested in furious self-advancement, greed and the pursuit of power for its own sake, is timeless. There is nothing new in the inanity of the sociopath and this is exemplified in the limited emotional and intellectual range

---

* In 2022 the University of Stoke put the infinite monkey theorem to the test at Flamingo Land. Confined for 48 hours, Jonathan Gullis not only produced five pages largely consisting of the letter 'S', but he also began to strike the keyboard with a stone, urinate and defecate on it.

of Shakespeare's Conservative characters. For these people, the accumulation of wealth, and the adrenaline of playing outside the rules, really is as good as it gets.

Shakespeare understood that the Tory's defining characteristic is his absence of imagination. Examples are the inability to grasp the intrinsic value of education on its own terms, the price paid for leaving a mutually beneficial union of your neighbours, or how many people will die if you fail to take timely action when threatened with a pandemic. When the closest thing they have to creative thought is only ever deployed in pursuit of wealth, it is cause for sympathy. Thus, when he finds that these stunted people can never experience wonder for its own sake, whether at the eternity of the heavens, a perplexing mathematical problem or the beguiling song of the blackbird, he invites us to pity the unpitiable.

It has been argued that the loss of *The Tragedie of the Tories* for so long made it inevitable its predictions would come to fruition. While this makes no sense, it does sound like the sort of thing an academic might say. It has also been argued that the events of the play have been repeated in real time, precisely because of the play's discovery. As Boris Johnson says in Act III Scene 3:

History's first law? I'm doomed to repeat it.

The character of Liz Truss has set challenges in performance. In 1997 Benedict Nightingale described Emma Thompson's portrayal (RSC) as 'the raving fever dream of an actress who has got too big for her boots and hasn't understood the assignment'. Of Franco Zeffirelli's 1962 film, Bamber Gascoigne declared her as 'clearly meant to fill the supernatural vacuum left behind by the Widdecombes upon Johnson's demise. Tippi Hedren's decision to play her straight is as fanciful as it was naïve. Such a woman could never become a prime minister, and therefore Truss is no cautionary tale, but a gratuitous embellishment that echoes *Titus* more than *Hamlet*.'

The fact, therefore, that Shakespeare's stark warning went unheeded, and that a woman matching Truss in both name and inanity went on to become prime minister and crash the UK economy, is a dark lesson for us all. And as we have just learnt, one we will ignore.

Shakespeare, while inviting compassion, held these portentous Tories in the highest disdain. In doing so, he remains, as ever, our contemporary.

DRAMATIS PERSONÆ

DAVID CAMERON, first leader of the Conservative Party
THERESA MAY, second leader of the Conservative Party
BORIS JOHNSON, third leader of the Conservative Party
LIZ TRUSS, fourth leader of the Conservative Party
RISHI SUNAK, fifth leader of the Conservative Party
DOMINIC CUMMINGS, a once-in-a-generation thinker
LEE CAIN, his sidekick
OLIVER LETWIN, Cameron's muse
DOMINIC RAAB, the hero of Kabul
JEREMY HUNT, luxury flat enthusiast
MICHAEL GOVE, a bivalve mollusc
JACOB REES-MOGG, an unserious person
MATTHEW HANCOCK, a parkour champion
OLIVER DOWDEN, a poltroon
PRITI PATEL, a dreadful person
SUELLA BRAVERMAN, a more dreadful person
ROBERT JENRICK, the pornographer's planning consultant
GRANT SHAPPS, MICHAEL GREEN, CORINNE STOCKHEATH, SEBASTIAN FOX, themselves
THÉRÈSE COFFEY, a volunteer abattoir worker
KWASI KWARTENG, Truss's muse

BEN BRADLEY, fodder
CHARLES WALKER, a milkman
ALEX STAFFORD, WENDY MORTON, MARK SPENCER, whips
GAVIN WILLIAMSON, has a whip
JAKE BERRY, thinks you should get a better job
MICHELLE DONELAN, taxpayer-funded defamer
PHILIP MAY, in love with THERESA MAY
CARRIE SYMONDS, in love with BORIS JOHNSON
NADINE DORRIES, really in love with BORIS JOHNSON
MAX HASTINGS, not in love with BORIS JOHNSON
ALLEGRA STRATTON, didn't get drunk with BORIS JOHNSON
NIMCO ALI, exempt from Covid restrictions
SIMON CASE, too ill to testify
DAVID FROST, once negotiated an extra sausage from a Ramada Inn buffet
JOHN BERCOW, the Speaker of the House
GRAHAM BRADY, the chair of the 1922 Committee
WILLIAM WRAGG, honey-trap victim
PHILIP HAMMOND, KEN CLARKE, AMBER RUDD, ANNA SOUBRY, DAVID GAUKE, RORY STEWART, NICHOLAS SOAMES, the Remainers
MARK FRANCOIS, DESMOND SWAYNE, STEVE BAKER, ANDREA LEADSOM, MICHAEL FABRICANT, the ERG
MARCUS RASHFORD, an effective politician
CHRIS WHITTY, a scientist
FRANÇOIS HOLLANDE, foreign
JEAN-CLAUDE JUNCKER, foreign
MICHEL BARNIER, foreign
DONALD TUSK, foreign

DRAMATIS PERSONÆ | 9

ANGELA MERKEL, foreign
URSULA VON DER LEYEN, foreign
BUREAUCRATS, unelected faceless ones, foreign
LAURA KUENSSBERG, NICK ROBINSON, ROBERT PESTON, EMILY MAITLIS, FIONA BRUCE, CAROLE MALONE, ALLISON PEARSON, HARRY COLE, NICK FERRARI, journalists
NIGEL FARAGE, grift horse
TOMMY ROBINSON, prodigal scum
ED MILIBAND, a leader of the opposition
JEREMY CORBYN, a leader of the opposition
KEIR STARMER, a leader of the opposition
SADIQ KHAN, the Mayor of London
LEE ANDERSON, the miner
MIRIAM CATES, the evangelical
NICK FLETCHER, the mediocre regional businessman
JONATHAN GULLIS, the PG Tips advert extra
BRENDAN CLARKE-SMITH, the supply teacher
MARK JENKINSON, the defender of statues
ANDREA JENKYNS, the finger-flicking yob
GREG HANDS, poor-man's Gordon Brittas
TICEANIA, queen of the Reform fairies
ISABEL OAKESHOTT, a fairy
LANCE FORMAN, a fairy
BEN HABIB, a fairy
DAVID BULL, a fairy
JUNE MUMMERY, a fairy
RED WALL, BORDER FORCE, ILLEGAL, characters in the Interlude performed by the clowns
STEVE BANNON, death
WIDDECOMBES, the Weïrd Sisters

THREE APPARITIONS OF CHRIS PINCHER, EVGENY LEBEDEV, A CHILD CROWNED WITH A BORIS HAIRDO
GHOSTS OF EDWARD HEATH, JOHN MAJOR, MRS THATCHER, TONY BLAIR, GORDON BROWN, NICK CLEGG
DOCTORS, NURSES, YOUNG TORIES, RIOTERS, POLICE, MESSENGERS, SPADS, AIDES, TV PRODUCER, GRAVEDIGGERS, others attending on senior Tories
CHORUS

ACT I

PROLOGUE

Enter CHORUS.

CHORUS
O, for a muse of fire that would ascend
The brightest heaven of pretention!
A kingdom for a stage, Tories to act,
Oligarchs to behold the swelling scene!
Then should the spamlike Cameron, himself,
Assume the sport of Tsars, and at his heels,
Leashed in like hounds, Sunak, Johnson, May, Truss
Crouch for employment. But pardon, voters all,
The cheap mulleted author that hath dared
On this unworthy scaffold to bring forth
So great an object. Can this hardback hold
The ghastly Westminster? Or may we cram
Within this dust jacket the very casques
That did affright the air at Downing Street?
O pardon, since a crookèd figure may
Attest in little place a million,
And let us, ciphers to this great account,
On your imaginary forces work.
Suppose within the girdle of these covers
Are now confined two Tory dynasties,
Whose high uprearèd and abutting fronts
The perilous narrow Brexit votes asunder.

Midst cold pensioners and warm horses, think:
Lies, incompetence, corruption and death,
For 'tis your thoughts that now must deck these crooks,
Carry them here and there, jumping o'er times,
Turning th' accomplishment of fourteen years
Into an hourglass; for the which supply,
Admit me chorus to this history,
Who, prologue-like, your humble patience pray
Gently to hear, kindly to judge this play.

SCENE I

An open Place.
Thunder and lightning. Enter three WIDDECOMBES.

FIRST WIDDECOMBE
　When shall we three meet again
　Big Brother, Strictly, Question Time?
SECOND WIDDECOMBE
　When Sky News' Kay Burley's on,
　When the battle's lost and won.
THIRD WIDDECOMBE
　We'll see it on the *News at One.*
FIRST WIDDECOMBE
　Where the place?
SECOND WIDDECOMBE
　On Hampstead Heath.
THIRD WIDDECOMBE
　There to meet with Johnson.

FIRST WIDDECOMBE
  I come, grey Larry!
SECOND WIDDECOMBE
  Money calls.
  Havoc calls.
THIRD WIDDECOMBE
  Anon.
ALL
  Fair is foul and foul is fair
  Hover through the fog and filthy air.

SCENE II

An air crash in a field in Kent.
Enter NIGEL FARAGE, a PARAMEDIC and a PILOT.

NIGEL FARAGE
  What country, friend, is this?
PARAMEDIC
  It's an ambulance, Nigel.
NIGEL FARAGE
  And what should I do in an ambulance?
  My career rests on winning South Thanet.
  Perchance we may still reach the Polling Station?
PARAMEDIC
  It is perchance that you yourself were sav'd.
NIGEL FARAGE
  O my poor career! and so perchance may it be.
PARAMEDIC
  True, Nigel: and, to comfort you with chance,

Assure yourself, after your plane did split,
When you, and that poor pilot sav'd with you,
Fell from the diving flight, the Border Force,
Most provident in peril, by myself
Were rung.

NIGEL FARAGE
For saying so, there's gold:
Mine own escape unfoldeth to my hope,
Whereto thy speech serves for reassurance,
Know'st thou this election day's result?

PARAMEDIC
Ay, Nigel, well; for I was following
To the rolling cov'rage on the BBC.

NIGEL FARAGE
Who governs now?

PARAMEDIC
An oily chap, in nature as in name.

NIGEL FARAGE
What is his name?

PARAMEDIC
Call him Dave.

NIGEL FARAGE
'Tis Cameron we have pinned Brexit on!
He has a majority?

PARAMEDIC
And so it seemed or did 'til very late;
For but an hour ago I turned it off,
And blue-lightèd to your crash – as, you know,
What exit polls tell, the rest prattle of –
But it did seem he'd won it fair and square.

NIGEL FARAGE
   What news.
PARAMEDIC
   And intriguing too, the longer went the count
   The more the Europe question: – leaving it
   The which we might regain Britain's sovereignty –
   Was foregrounded; and through this dear game,
   They say, Dave hath destroyed the Lib Dems
   And Labour too.
NIGEL FARAGE
   Presently, I must to the BBC.
   My hatred undelivered to the world,
   Till I had made them think what a good fellow
   This xenophobe is.
PARAMEDIC
   That were hard to compass,
   Because they will admit no kind of suit,
   Not balanced.
NIGEL FARAGE
   Trust me, I'll play them for fools.
   There is a fair behaviour in thee, 'medic;
   And though that nature with you NHS staff
   Doth oft close in pollution, yet of thee
   I will believe thou hast a mind that suits
   A proud and patriotic character.
PARAMEDIC
   Good, because you need sutures. Fifty-two.
NIGEL FARAGE
   I prithee, and I'll pay thee bounteously,
   Recover me what I am, then call the Beeb:

Thou shalt present me as tenable to them;
It may be worth thy pains, for I can sing
And speak to them in many sorts of music
That will allow me very worth their service.
What else may hap, to time I will commit;
Only shape thou silence to my wit.

PARAMEDIC
Be they your soft marks, and your mute I'll be;
When my tongue blabs, then let mine eyes not see.

NIGEL FARAGE
I thank thee; sew me up. *Exeunt.*

SCENE III

Westminster.
Enter DAVID CAMERON, *the Prime Minister, solus.*

DAVID CAMERON
Now is the winter of our discontent
Made glorious summer by *The Sun*'s News Corp;
And all the clouds that lour'd upon our house
In the deep bosom of Levinson are buried.
Now are our brows bound with victorious wreaths;
Our hackèd phones hung up by columnists;
Our negative campaign has Labour deposed,
Our Lib Dem partners all now unseated.
Grim-visaged Murdoch soothes with tabloid font;
And now, instead of mounting barbed leads
To taint the souls of fearful adversaries,
We caper'd nimbly by Ed's renownèd Stone,
To the pleasant sound of bacon sarnie gaffes.

ACT I, SCENE III | 17

But I, that incline to austerity,
Nor bothered to support a fragile working class;
I, that am roundly flanked by these Bullingdon sons,
Now cozy up to my Eurosceptic fringe.
I, that was blessed of this Rupert's backing,
Cheating your future by dissembling nature,
Entitled, indifferent, Etonian true,
Born to reign, breeding pure, rare elite pup.
And thus, so pervasively out of touch,
That babies cry as I halt to kiss them;
Why, I, with mandate for this time of peace,
Have no delight to pass away the time,
Unless to see my shadow in *The Sun*.
Descanting on mine known indifference:
And therefore, since I cannot find a reason
To entertain more fair untroubled days,
I determined am to fix the Tories
And sate the sectist Brexit devotees.
Plans have I laid, to Brussels will I go,
There to renegotiate England's place.
To set the forbearing and the right wing
In deadly spite the one against the other:
And if the hopeful be as true and just
As they are subtle, false and treacherous,
This day should England be divided up,
About referendum, which says we;
Of optimism's heir shall soon be free.
Dive, thoughts, down to Wapping: here
Red Ed comes.
        Enter ED MILIBAND, *guarded by* KEIR STARMER.
Brother, good day. What means this armed guard
That waits upon your Grace?

ED MILIBAND
   Our membership,
   Tend'ring my person's safety, hath appointed
   This conduct to convey me to the Tower.

DAVID CAMERON
   Upon what cause?

ED MILIBAND
   Because my name is Ed.

DAVID CAMERON
   Alack, my lord, that fault is none of yours.
   Do they seize Murphy and Van Halen too?
   Or, belike the membership hath some intent
   That you should be new-christened in the Tower.
   But what's the reason, Edward? May I know?

ED MILIBAND
   Yea, young Dave, when I know, for I protest
   I do not. As I can learn, Team Corbyn
   Does hearken after prophecies and dreams,
   And from the cross-row plucks the letter E,
   And says a wizard told them that by 'E'
   The movement disinherited should be.
   And for my name of Ed begins with E,
   It follows in their thought that I am he.
   These, as I learn, and such like toys as these,
   Hath moved the members to depose me now.

DAVID CAMERON
   This it is when men are by Momentum ruled.
   'Tis not members that send you to the Tower;
   But the syndicalists, Edward, 'tis they
   That temper him to this extremity.
   The Liberal Democrats did of late,
   For failure, send Clegg to San Francisco

From whence this present day he is delivered,
By Facebook. So do not be sad, Miliband.
Your future in data harvests might land.

ED MILBAND
By heaven, I think there is none more sure
Than Zuckerberg's kindred, whose tech start-ups
Do thrive in Valleys made of Silicon.
Heard you not what an humble suppliant
Young Nick was to him for delivery?

DAVID CAMERON
Humbly appealing to his deity
Got my ex-Deputy his liberty.
But tell you what: I think it is the way,
That you should with Jeremy keep on side.
To be his man and draw your salary.
Ere jealous o'erworn Euroscepticism,
That for my career I risk our realm's fate,
Brings mighty problems to the polity.

KEIR STARMER
I beseech your Graces both to pardon me.
But Seumas Milne hath straitly given in charge
That no man shall have private conference,
Of what degree soever, with this comrade.

DAVID CAMERON
E'en so; an it please your worship, Sir Keir,
You may partake of anything we, the
The natural party of government, say.
And we say that Ed ran a campaign bland.
One which lost to our negativity.
Yes, hoodies I hugged and gays I let wed
But arrant nationalism returned us,

Unshackled from our Lib Dem albatross.
How say you, Keir? Can you deny all this?

KEIR STARMER
With this, my lord, myself have naught to do.

DAVID CAMERON
Naught to do with politics? I tell thee, fellow,
He that doth naught else but keep his head down
Inclines to make plots secretly, alone.

KEIR STARMER
I know not what statecraft implies your Grace,
And withal, forbear your conference with Miliband.

ED MILIBAND
I know thy charge, Keir Starmer, and will obey.

DAVID CAMERON
We are the Queen's abjects and must obey.
Red Ed, farewell. I will unto the Queen,
And beseech her to form a government.
Then referendum I'll call. In or out
I will perform it to enfranchise few
Bar my own prospects, and CCHQ.

ED MILIBAND
I know. It pleaseth neither of us well.

DAVID CAMERON
Well, your imprisonment shall not be long.
I will deliver Remain just for you.
Have patience.

ED MILIBAND
I must perforce. Farewell, Dave.

Exeunt MILIBAND, STARMER and GUARD.

DAVID CAMERON
Go tread the path that thou shalt ne'er return.
Oh simple, stupid Ed, I do love thee.

Since we sold Chaos with Ed Miliband
Her Maj calls forth Dave to be her right hand.
But who comes here? *Enter MICHAEL GOVE.*

MICHAEL GOVE

Good time of the day, David, my good lord.

DAVID CAMERON

As much unto my good Lord Michael Gove.
Well are you welcome to the open air.
Tell me, Mike, how hath the back benches brooked?

MICHAEL GOVE

With patience, David, as hostages must;
But I shall live, David, to give them thanks
That, David, did my relegation cause.

DAVID CAMERON

No doubt, no doubt, the Eurosceptics too.
For that they were my enemies, but now,
I'll prevail upon them as much as you.

MICHAEL GOVE

More pity that the exports should be mewed,
Whiles boffs and experts prey at liberty.

DAVID CAMERON

What news abroad?

MICHAEL GOVE

None so bad, David, as this: Farage, Nige
Has had a brush with death. An air crash.
And for him, mightily physicians fear.

DAVID CAMERON

Now, by Delors, indeed that news is bad.
O, now he hath flown too close to the sun,
His ambition, consumed with sovereignty.
'Tis very tragic to be thinking on.
Go before, Mike, and I will follow you. *Exit GOVE.*

He cannot live, I hope, so Brexit dies
With UKIP back to Deal and Margate packed.
I'll feign to park my tanks on Nigel's lawn
Use lies well steeled with weighty arguments;
And, if I fail not in my intent deep,
Brexit hath not another day to live;
Which done, God take old Farage to his end,
And leave the world for me to bustle in.
For then I'll reign the Eurosceptic fringe.
I run to open market ere my horse.
While Nige breathes, the eyes swivelled enthral us.
When they are gone, then must I count my gains.

SCENE IV

Hampstead Heath.
Enter WIDDECOMBES.

ALL
Fair is foul, and foul is fair:
Hover through the fog and filthy air.
FIRST WIDDECOMBE
Where hast thou been, sister?
SECOND WIDDECOMBE
Jeremy Vine.
THIRD WIDDECOMBE
Look what I have.
SECOND WIDDECOMBE
Show me, show me.

FIRST WIDDECOMBE
  Here I have a scrounger's thumb,
  Wreck'd as homeward he did come. *Drum within.*
THIRD WIDDECOMBE
  A drum, a drum!
  Johnson doth come.
          Enter BORIS JOHNSON *and* DOMINIC CUMMINGS.
BORIS JOHNSON
  So fouleroonie day I have not seen.
DOMINIC CUMMINGS
  How far is't Barnard Castle? What are these
  So wither'd and so wild in their attire,
  Who look not like the STEM boys and tech bros,
  That I'm used to. Live you? or are you aught
  That man may question? You seem to understand me
  By each at once her choppy finger laying
  Upon her skinny lips. You should be women,
  And yet your beards forbid me to interpret
  That you are so.
BORIS JOHNSON
  By jingo, speak, if you can. What are you?
FIRST WIDDECOMBE
  All hail, Johnson! hail to thee, Thane of Lies!
SECOND WIDDECOMBE
  All hail, Johnson, hail to thee, Thane of Brexit!
THIRD WIDDECOMBE
  All hail, Johnson, thou shalt be PM after!
DOMINIC CUMMINGS
  Why, Boris, do you start, and seem to fear
  Such polling data when it sounds so fair?

You greet with great forecasts and predictions
Of power grabbing and of Brexit hope,
That he seems rapt withal. To me you speak not.
If you can look into the seeds of time,
And say which grain will grow my Substack blog,
Speak then to aloof Dom, who never begs,
Nor fears your favours or your weirdo games.

FIRST WIDDECOMBE
 Hail!
SECOND WIDDECOMBE
 Hail!
THIRD WIDDECOMBE
 Hail!
FIRST WIDDECOMBE
 Lesser than Johnson, and greater.
SECOND WIDDECOMBE
 Not so weird, yet much weirder.
THIRD WIDDECOMBE
 Thou, eight-bit shaman, shall be disruptor
 Of the deep-Deep State status quo
 So all hail, Johnson and Cummings!
FIRST WIDDECOMBE
 Cummings and Johnson, all hail!
BORIS JOHNSON
 Stay, you imperfect speakers, tell me more:
 By Stringfellow I know I'm Thane of Lies;
 But how of Brexit? Cameron still leads,
 The latex-faced tosser; but yes, PM
 Stands well within the prospect of belief,
 No less than to be World King. Say from
    whence

You owe this strange intelligence? or why
Upon this blasted Heath you stop our way
With such prophetic greeting? I charge you:
Spaff! *WIDDECOMBES vanish.*

DOMINIC CUMMINGS
Whither are they vanish'd?

BORIS JOHNSON
Not since my concealment in wardrobe last
Has a grotesque shape vanish'd in such haste.
Would they had stay'd!

DOMINIC CUMMINGS
Were such things here as we do speak about?

BORIS JOHNSON
You shall disrupt.

DOMINIC CUMMINGS
You shall rule us.

BORIS JOHNSON
And Thane of Brexit too. Went it not so?

DOMINIC CUMMINGS
To the self-same tune and words. *Exeunt.*

SCENE V

A bar.
Enter NICK ROBINSON and LAURA KUENSSBERG.

NICK ROBINSON
After the election, the changes I perceived in Cameron and
 Clegg were very notes of desolation. They seemed almost,
 with staring on one another, to tear the cases of their eyes.

There was speech in their dumbness, language in their very gesture; they looked as they had heard of a world ransomed, or one destroyed. A notable passion of wonder appeared in them; but the wisest beholder, that knew no more but seeing, could not say if th' importance were joy or sorrow; but in the extremity of the one, it must needs be.

LAURA KUENSSBERG
Beseech you, sir, were you present at this relation?

NICK ROBINSON
I was by at the counting of the ballots, and heard old Dimbleby deliver the manner how he found it.

LAURA KUENSSBERG
I would most gladly know the issue of it.

NICK ROBINSON
I make a broken delivery of the business; here comes ITV's budget Poindexter Robert Peston, that happily knows more. *Enter ROBERT PESTON.*
The news, Robert?

ROBERT PESTON
Nothing but bonfires: the oracle is fulfilled: the referendum is called: such a deal of wonder is broken out within this hour that ballad-makers cannot be able to express it. Here comes *Newsnight*'s Emily Maitlis. She can deliver you more. *Enter EMILY MAITLIS.*
How goes it now, ma'am? This news, which is called true, is so like an old tale that the verity of it is in strong suspicion. Has Cameron called it on?

EMILY MAITLIS
Most true, if ever truth were pregnant by circumstance. That which you hear you'll swear you see, there is such unity in

the proofs: The United Kingdom's fate is to be contested, betwixt the vested greed of disaster capitalists, and avocado-dependent elites whose nature has been repeatedly shown to be intrinsically annoying. Illegal data-harvesting techniques will confront appeals to a reviled status quo and this, and many other confirmations beside, proclaim, with all certainty, that it will be a shit show. Did you hear about Farage?

LAURA KUENSSBERG
No.

EMILY MAITLIS
Then you have missed an incident which had to be seen and cannot be spoken of, for there was a casting up of eyes and holding up of hands with countenances of immense distraction when Nigel's two-seater PZL-104 tangled with the UKIP banner it was trailing and fell from the sky. Cameron, being ready to leap out of himself for joy, thinking his biggest problem departed, now embraces the vote he cannot afford to lose.

ROBERT PESTON
What, pray you, became of him that crashed hence this plane?

EMILY MAITLIS
Like an old tale still, which will have matter to rehearse, though credit be asleep and not an ear open. He lives. This was avouched me by a paramedic who has not only his innocence, which seems much, to justify him, but a UKIP membership card.

LAURA KUENSSBERG
Then we must immediately hear more from Nigel.

ROBERT PESTON
Are the divisions formed?
EMILY MAITLIS
The battle buses are rolling. Those that would voluntarily impose trade sanctions upon us are led by Cummings and fed by Banks, with Gove, Villiers, IDS and Francois in strong suit. The defenders of GDP – Cameron, Truss, Major and Blair – are a team so insipid, they would beguile Nature of her will to live. Thither with all greediness of affection are they all gone to bicker. Consensus has fled and is replaced with beef, about bananas.
ROBERT PESTON
And what of the mayor, Johnson?
EMILY MAITLIS
He has denied to fight yet, but they say, when his allegiance he declares, many millions will be seduced by his babble.
ROBERT PESTON
I thought we had some great matter there in hand; for I hath privately twice or thrice a day, ever since the global financial crisis, wondered at the future of our moribund politics. If Johnson is it, we are done for. Shall we thither and with our company record the campaigning?
EMILY MAITLIS
Our absence makes us unthrifty to our knowledge. Let's along. *Exeunt JOURNALISTS.*
LAURA KUENSSBERG
Now I, having the dash of the careerist in me, hope preferment will drop on my head. With softballs and gentle questions I shall bring these legislators to my table; talk of customs unions, but press them on football teams. While the populous become sick of the word Brexit, the

extremities of their passions will remain undiscover'd, I shall tap 'sources close to the prime minister'. 'Tis all one to me; for had I been required to probe, I would not have relish'd among my prospects.   *Exit* KUENSSBERG.

SCENE VI

DOMINIC CUMMINGS
How goes the night, boy?
SUPER-TALENTED WEIRDO
The web is down; I have not heard the clock.
DOMINIC CUMMINGS
And she goes down at twelve.
SUPER-TALENTED WEIRDO
I take't, 'tis outage, sir.
DOMINIC CUMMINGS
Hold, take my Mac. There's husbandry in BT;
Their broadband is all out. Take thee that too.
A heavy summons lies like lead on me,
And yet I would not sleep. Disruptive powers
Restrain in me the mundane thoughts that nature
Gives way to in others.
   Enter BORIS JOHNSON *and an* IT CONSULTANT
   with a torch.
Give me my Mac. Who's there?
BORIS JOHNSON
The guest host of *Have I Got News for You*.
DOMINIC CUMMINGS
Boris, not at rest? Cameron's abroad:
He is in unusual pleasure and

Sends forth great largess to your offices.
A cabinet role greets your personage,
By name of Remain's broker, to shut up
Your leadership bids.

BORIS JOHNSON
Being undeclared,
I'll pretend to serve Dave's doomed endeavour
Which then shall I but wreck.

DOMINIC CUMMINGS
Disruption. I love it.
I dreamt last night of the three Widdecombes:
To you they have show'd some truth.

BORIS JOHNSON
Those tank-topped bum boys? I think not of them:
Yet, when we can entreat an hour to serve,
We might spend it in some words on my own
Ambitions, if you would grant the time twixt
Your civil service feather-rustling sports.

DOMINIC CUMMINGS
At your kind'st leisure.

BORIS JOHNSON
If you shall cling to my consent, when 'tis,
It shall make honour for you.

DOMINIC CUMMINGS
So I lose none
In seeking to augment it, if we keep
With Brexit franchis'd, and allegiance clear,
We rulers shall be.

BORIS JOHNSON
Good repose the while!

DOMINIC CUMMINGS
  I'm too smart to sleep: but the like to you.
        Exeunt CUMMINGS *and* SUPER-TALENTED WEIRDO.
BORIS JOHNSON
  Go prepare my lesson. Fetch lingerie,
  Help me to spread my sheets. Get thee to bed.
                              Exit IT CONSULTANT.
                    JOHNSON *puts down a laptop case.*
  Is this a blagger which I see before me,
  New column toward my mind? Come, let me write thee:
  I write thee not, and yet I write thee still.
  Art thou not, fatal column, sensible
  To Remain as to Leave? or art thou but
  Word doc of the mind, a false creation,
  Proceeding from the heat-oppressed brain?
  I see thee yet, in form as palpable
  As this which now I draw.
              He begins to take the laptop out of its case.
  Thou marshall'st me the way that I was going;
  And such an instrument I was to use.
  Mine words are made the fools o' the other Leavers,
  Or else worth all the rest: I type thee still;
  And through thy QWERTY keyboard, doubt does flood,
  Which was not so before. There's no such thing.
  It is the Brexit business which informs
  This hesitance. Now o'er the one half-land
  Reason seems dead, and silly hopes abuse
  The UK's peace. Team Leave advocates
  With Murdoch, Barclay Bros and Rothermere
  And their sentinels, *Sun, Telegraph, Mail,*

Poisonous nostalgia and UKIP lies,
Propelling fools with gold towards false designs
Of village greens and sepia high streets,
Hear not my keystrokes, which way I type, lest
The very keys prate of my intention.
I'll write two columns, hedging for the *Times*,
Which one suits me best? One remains, one leaves.
Words to the heat of deeds too cold breath gives.

A bell rings.

I go, and it is done. The bell invites me.
Hear it not, Cameron, it is a knell
That summons thee to heaven or to hell.

SCENE VII

*A field near Chipping Norton, the eve of the Brexit referendum.
Enter DAVID CAMERON in arms, with GEORGE OSBORNE,
LIZ TRUSS and OLIVER LETWIN with others.*

DAVID CAMERON
Here pitch our tent. From Chipping Norton's fields
We'll command the votes of our citizens.
George Osborne, why look you so sad?

GEORGE OSBORNE
That's just austerity's architect's face,
Drained of life, like the ailing I make work.
My heart is ten times lighter than my looks.

DAVID CAMERON
Liz Truss of Norfolk.

LIZ TRUSS
Here, most gracious liege.

DAVID CAMERON
 Ms Truss, we must have knock, ha, must we not?
LIZ TRUSS
 Yes, for our pork and cheese markets, we must.
DAVID CAMERON
 Up with my yurt! Here will I lie this night.
 But where tomorrow? Well, all's one for that.
 Who hath descried the number of Vote Leave?
GEORGE OSBORNE
 The early polling data looks good.
 Six, seven mil is their utmost turnout.
DAVID CAMERON
 A million votes change? That's a lot, George.
 Still, suburban Remainers edge that count.
 And Cameron's name is a spire of strength
 Which they upon the Brexit faction want.
 Up with my pod! Come, colleagues complacent,
 Let us survey the vantage of the ground.
 Call Soho House and fetch me a hot tub.
 Let's lack no decadence, make no delay,
 For, lords, tomorrow is a busy day.
            The glamping pod is now ready. Exeunt.
Enter BORIS JOHNSON, MICHAEL GOVE, CAROLE MALONE, HARRY
      COLE *and* LEE CAIN *who parks* CUMMINGS' *motorhome.*
BORIS JOHNSON
 The brazen *Sun* will make a headline gold,
 And by the track of Dacre's fiery *Mail*
 A token of a spiffing day tomorrow.
 In Britain 'BeLEAVE'. Who says print is dead?
 Young Harry Cole, you shall bear the standard.
 Give Cummings whiteboard, laser pen and ears;
 He'll draw the form and model of the plan. Dom?

DOMINIC CUMMINGS
  Set out, each journalist, your tabloid's line,
  And print in propaganda clear our lies.
  Paul Dacre, Hartley-Brewer, Harry Cole,
  And you, Ms Carole Malone, stay with me.
  Yon Sarah Vine fires her barbs flawlessly. –
  Odd Michael Gove, bear my goodnight to her,
  And by the second hour in the morning
  Desire your Amazon visit my tent.
  One thing more, slimy Michael, do for me.
  Where is yon Corbyn quartered, do you know?

MICHAEL GOVE
  Unless I have mista'en his colours much,
  Which well I am assured I could have done,
  His sentiment lies in Islington north,
  An avocado consumption hot spot.

DOMINIC CUMMINGS
  If without peril it be possible,
  Sweet oozing Gove, make means to speak with him,
  And give him from me this most needful note.
          He slips a note inside a copy of Mao's Little Red Book.

MICHAEL GOVE
  Upon my life, my lord, I'll undertake it;
  I do live for these tawdry escapades.

DOMINIC CUMMINGS
  Good night, Michael Gove.   *Exit* GOVE.

BORIS JOHNSON
  You bivalve mollusc.

DOMINIC CUMMINGS
  Come, 'journalists',
  Let us consult upon tomorrow's business;

ACT I, SCENE VII

Into Dom's breakout space. The dew is raw.
  JOURNALISTS *withdraw into the tent. The others exeunt.*
    Enter to his glamping pod DAVID CAMERON,
      THERESA MAY, GEORGE OSBORNE,
      LIZ TRUSS *and* OLIVER LETWIN *with others.*

DAVID CAMERON
  What is't o'clock?
GEORGE OSBORNE
  It's supper time, my lord. It's nine o'clock.
DAVID CAMERON
  I'll sup well tonight. Get me Chardonnay.
  Some uramaki sushi. And oysters.
  Is my silk kimono laid on the bed?
GEORGE OSBORNE
  It is, Dave, all things are in readiness.
DAVID CAMERON
  Good Liz Truss, hie thee to thy charge;
  Have you got a crayon stuck up your nose?
LIZ TRUSS
  Yes, it's Red. In case we have to draw blood.
DAVID CAMERON
  Stir with the lark tomorrow, simple Liz Truss.
LIZ TRUSS
  I'm a politics.   *Exit.*
DAVID CAMERON
  Theresa May!
THERESA MAY
  My liege.
DAVID CAMERON
  Send out some dithering backbench no-mark
  To Johnson's battle bus. Bid them do it

For cause Remaining, lest their career fall
Into the blind cave of eternal night.
THERESA MAY
Hancock. *Exit* MAY.
DAVID CAMERON
Fill me my bath with salts. Fetch my face mask.
My Audi valet, moisturise my hands.
I do not wish to appear out of touch.
Letwin!
OLIVER LETWIN
My lord?
DAVID CAMERON
Saw'st thou the melancholy git Ken Clarke?
OLIVER LETWIN
Yes. Dave Gauke, Anna Soubry and suave Ken
Have been on the switchboards, and call to call
They with charm, hope to floating voters sway.
DAVID CAMERON
So, I'm satisfied. Find a detox juice.
I've refinèd my metabolism,
Through focussing on macronutrients.
Set it down. Is my sashimi ready?
OLIVER LETWIN
It is, my lord.
DAVID CAMERON
Bid my guard watch; leave me.
And Letwin, about midnight visit me.
Bring my pilates mat.
Exit LETWIN. CAMERON *withdraws into his pod; aides guard it.*
Enter JEREMY CORBYN *to* DOMINIC CUMMINGS *in his RV.*
JEREMY CORBYN

Good evening, this isn't a trap is it?
BORIS JOHNSON
Nooooo, Jeremy Corbyn.
JEREMY CORBYN
Sounds reasonable.
DOMININC CUMMINGS
All comfort moral certainty can give.
Tell me, how fares thy noble comrades, Jez?
JEREMY CORBYN
I, by attorney, from my comrades greet,
Who will end neoliberalism's yoke,
By routinely walking into their snares.
In brief, for so old Seumas bids me be,
My fortune I'll to the arbitrement
Of xenophobes and metric-hating bores.
I, as I may – that which I would I can't –
Will implicitly support Brexit's claim,
And aid thee in this spasm nostalgic.
On thy side I may not too forward be,
Lest, being seen, my fragile consensus,
Be executed by the Labour right.
So long; this discourse and the fearful time
Risks blowing my wider socialist plan.
My enemy's enemy is my friend,
Campaigning weakly, my means to an end.
BORIS JOHNSON
Good Jezza, plainly, you've done the right thing.
We promise we'll play fair next election,
No anti-Semitism, smears or no,
Will you see shamelessly leveraged by
My institutionally racist friends.

I'll strive with brain box here to take a nap,
Lest leaden slumber peise old Bozzy down
When I should mount with wings of victory!
Once more, it's time for a slumberaroony.
Onwards.

Exit CORBYN. JOHNSON *sleeps.*
Enter the GHOST OF EDWARD HEATH.

GHOST OF EDWARD HEATH   *To* CAMERON:
Let me sit heavy on thy soul tomorrow.
Think how thou betray my greatest achievement:
Our membership of the Common Market.

To JOHNSON:
Moron.   *Exit.*
Enter the GHOST OF JOHN MAJOR.

GHOST OF JOHN MAJOR   *To* CAMERON:
Let me sit heavy in thy soul tomorrow,
I, whose ratification of Maastricht
Is by thy rank guile betrayed for fame.
All those lost hours with Norma; squandered.

To JOHNSON:
You are a tosser.   *Exit.*
Enter the GHOST OF MRS THATCHER.

GHOST OF MRS THATCHER   *To* CAMERON:
When I was mortal, my anointed frame
Was revered throughout the continent all.
Think on the rebate and me. Despair, Dave;
Mags Thatcher bids thy career will now die.

To JOHNSON:
Twat.   *Exit.*
Enter the GHOSTS OF TONY BLAIR, GORDON BROWN
and NICK CLEGG.

ACT I, SCENE VII | 39

GHOST OF TONY BLAIR *To* CAMERON:
  Let me sit heavy in thy soul tomorrow,
  Tone that won landslide. More Thatcherite than thee.
  To JOHNSON:
  I've got a bridge to sell you.
GHOST OF BROWN *To* CAMERON:
  Think upon Brown, in the shadow of Blair.
  A poor man's Nick Clegg. I loathed every bit.
  To JOHNSON:
  I've got a fridge to sell you.
GHOST OF NICK CLEGG *To* CAMERON:
  Think upon Clegg, 'It's not you, Nick, it's me.'
  Gross liar. Think on Meta, despair and die!
  To JOHNSON:
  Sighs.
  Exeunt.
  CAMERON *starts up out of his dream.*
DAVID CAMERON
  Get me a shepherd's hut! Lock its twee doors!
  Nick, it was me, not you! Soft! I did dream.
  O coward conscience, how thou afflicts me!
  Cold fearful drops stand on my trembling flesh.
  What do I fear? Brexit? There's no cause why.
  David loves David, that is, I am I.
  I am no villain that I tried to heal us,
  To unite Tories. But if it not pass.
  My conscience hath a thousand several tongues,
  And every tongue brings in a several tale,
  And every tale in Chipping Norton ends.
  Chardonnay, Chardonnay, with 'Bekah and
    Charlie;

Dinner, nice, dinner with Clarkson makes three;
With artisan gins, not one nobody,
Throng we the bar, these Cotswold A-listees!
Methought the souls of all whose ends I derailed
Came to my pod, and every one did threat
Tomorrow's vengeance on my head. Idiots.

Enter OLIVER LETWIN.

OLIVER LETWIN
My lord!
DAVID CAMERON
Zounds! Who's there?
OLIVER LETWIN
Oliver Letwin; Soho House's cock
Hath twice done salutation to the morn;
The nation is up and heading to polls.
DAVID CAMERON
O Letwin, I have dreamed a vivid dream!
What think'st thou, will Remainers prove all
  true?
OLIVER LETWIN
No idea, my lord.
DAVID CAMERON
O Letwin, I can't be arsed!
OLIVER LETWIN
Nay, good my lord, be not afraid of defeat.
DAVID CAMERON
By Scargill's elbow pads, I am not.
I now see for the first time in my life
That there is more to life than politics.
Armed in proof, by how little I care now.
'Tis not yet near day. Come, go with me.
Outside this yurt I'll play ukulele.

ACT I, SCENE VII | 41

My Sam Cam has a dolphin tattoo blue,
Now it's Dave Cam's turn to find himself too.
Exeunt CAMERON *and* LETWIN *with ukuleles.*
Enter COLUMNISTS *to* JOHNSON *in his tent.*

ALLISON PEARSON
Good morrow, Boris.

BORIS JOHNSON
Cry mercy, ghouls, shills and journalists,
That you have ta'en a tardy sluggard here.

HARRY COLE
How have you slept, my lord?

BORIS JOHNSON
The sweetest sleep and fairest-boding dreams
That ever entered a blond tousled bonce
Have I since your departure had, my friends.
The souls of grandees like Major and Heath
Came to my tent and had great sport with me
I promise you, my heart is very jolly
In its remembrance. It happens most nights.
How far into the morning is it, lords?

CAROLE MALONE
Upon the stroke of noon.

BORIS JOHNSON
Why, 'tis time to dress and give direction.
His oration to his supporters:
More than I have said, loving patriots,
The leisure and enforcement of the time
Forbids to dwell upon. Yet remember this:
For Brexit's cause, God fights upon on our side;
The data of northern plebs and wrong'd proles,
From Cambridge Analytica is bought.
Cameron except, those whom we vote 'gainst

Had rather Labour win than him who fails.
For what is he they follow? Truly, chaps,
A privileged Etonian dandy;
One birthed by blood, to wealth and affluence;
One that was into power and means born,
Thus contrasting BoJo, the people's prince,
And working classeroonie, earthy foil
To Cameron's privilege, so false set;
One that hath ever been the grafter's friend.
Fight with me against entitlement blithe
God will, in justice, ward you patriots;
If you do sweat to help take control back,
You'll sleep in peace, the EU being slain;
If you do fight against your country's foes,
Your NHS shall get three hundred mil;
If you do fight in safeguard of your seas,
Our trawlermen and fish shall happy be;
If farmers you do from their exports free,
Replacing some red tape, with even more.
Your children's children will sanctify you.
Then, in the name of God and all these rights,
Go to the polls, X your preferrèd box.
For me, the ransom of my bold attempt
Shall be a broadsheet column – chicken feed;
But if I thrive, this gain of sovereignty,
The least of you shall bathe in upland sun.
Sound 'Rule, Britannia'! boldly and cheerfully!
Saint George and freedom! Boris's victory! *Exeunt.*
        Enter DAVID CAMERON, OLIVER LETWIN *and others.*
DAVID CAMERON
What said Rory Stewart regarding Johnson?

OLIVER LETWIN
  That he was but an utter charlatan.
DAVID CAMERON
  He said the truth. And what said Ken Clarke then?
OLIVER LETWIN
  He yawned, and said, 'Yes, boy. Fetch my Hush Puppies.'
DAVID CAMERON
  He was in the right, and so indeed he is.

The clock striketh.

  Tell the clock there. Give me a calendar.
  Who saw *The Sun* today?
OLIVER LETWIN
  Not I, my lord.
DAVID CAMERON
  Look here. 'BeLEAVE in Britain', by the book
  Where is our favourable coverage?
  A brown nose I have from nuzzling Rupert's arse.
  Hancock!

Enter MATT HANCOCK.

MATT HANCOCK
  I wasn't snogging my aide.
DAVID CAMERON
  What did Johnson say?
MATT HANCOCK
  Sorry, I forgot to ask.
DAVID CAMERON
  Go, Hancock, find out.
  Come, bustle! Come caparison my hut.
  I will go to vote. But if we then lose,
  A lengthy all-inclusive will I brave: *Enter LIZ TRUSS.*

LIZ TRUSS
 We import two-thirds of our cheese.
DAVID CAMERON
 Then bid a cheese board sought from Alex James.
>> *She sheweth him a paper.*

LIZ TRUSS
 This found I on my tent this morning.
DAVID CAMERON *Reads:*
 'Lizzie of Norfolk, be not too bereft.
 For the West has but eighteen years left.'
 An enemy ploy to confuse you.
 Go, Remainers, each to his voting booth.
 Lest not your bubbling oatmilk lattes chill.
 Conscience is but a word that cowards use,
 Devised at first to stop us having fun.
 Let comfort be our conscience, ease our law.
 March on, smarmily. Let us to it pell-mell,
 If not to heaven, then a luxury hotel.
>> *His oration to team Remain:*
 What shall I say more than I have implied?
 Remember who you're voting 'gainst, and why.
 These vagabonds, rascals and layabouts,
 The scum of Britain, northern peasants' base,
 Whom their o'er-cloyèd counties vomit forth,
 Like unhinged *Emmerdale* and *Corrie* plots.
 You sleeping safe, they bring to Zone 2, strife;
 You having chic, metropolitan lives,
 They'll make it harder to take holidays,
 And what doth lead them but this sovereignty,
 Long kept in Brussels for a rainy day.
 These uncouth louts, that never in their lives
 Did any work but on bleak Asda tills.

Let's whip these stragglers back up the A1
Lash hence these overweening rags of Leeds,
These shirker Scousers, jealous of our lives,
Who, but for dreaming on this exploit daft,
For want of means, poor rats, watch rugby league!
If we be conquered, let bankers do it,
And not these Brexiting, minimum-wage,
Fried, green-eyed, left-behind belligerents,
Who choose Doncaster over Kensington.
Shall these enjoy our lands? Mess up our lives,
Ravish our pensions?
    'Land of Hope and Glory' being played on a kazoo
                afar off.
Hark, I hear their drum.
Vote, Remainers of England! Elite, vote!
Vote, urbane, smug, out of touch homeowners!
Start your proud Beamers, drive, double-park, vote!
Vanquish the lowborn, with entitlement!
            Enter a MESSENGER.
What says Lord Johnson? Will he bring his power?

MESSENGER
 My lord, he doth deny to come.

DAVID CAMERON
 Then off with his son's head!

OLIVER LETWIN
 My liege, he has too many. He won't care.

DAVID CAMERON
 A thousand thoughts are now within my bosom.
 Advise my agent. Warn my publisher.
 Our ancient land of courage, fair Saint George,
 Will lose five per cent of his GDP.
 Upon which retreat must I to safety.   *Exeunt.*

SCENE VIII

Westminster.
Alarum. Excursions. Enter OLIVER LETWIN *and*
AIDES; *to him* GEORGE OSBORNE.

GEORGE OSBORNE
   The pound is tanking! Jeremy Vine said,
   From his CGI-rendered Downing Street,
   That in Sunderland they've just voted leave.
OLIVER LETWIN
   Where is the architect of this shit show?
GEORGE OSBORNE
   Brave Dave fearlessly seeks his shepherd's hut.
   His hopes are slain, and he already looks
   For suitable early retirement spots.
                              Alarum. Enter DAVID CAMERON.
DAVID CAMERON
   A hut! A hut! My kingdom for a hut!
GEORGE OSBORNE
   Withdraw, my lord; We'll help you find a hut.
DAVID CAMERON
   Sure. I have set my life upon a cast,
   But I'll stand the hazard of the die.
   I think there be shepherds' huts in this field;
   Five have I seen today that look quite smart.
   A hut! A hut! My kingdom for a hut.   *Exeunt.*

ACT II

PROLOGUE

Enter CHORUS.

CHORUS
  Now all brokers of England are on fire,
  And Boris's dalliance in the wardrobe lies.
  Now thrive the hedge funders. And Brexit's thought
  Reigns solely in the breast of every man,
  These Sunlit Uplands now did hire the vote.
  Following the mirror of Conservative kings,
  With singèd heels, Cameron is deposed.
  And now sits Mrs May in Number Ten,
  Where parliament is hung unto the point,
  With landslide victory, crowns and Corbyn's head
  Promis'd to Tories and their followers,
  She is advis'd by bad intelligence,
  To send the nation back to ballot box,
  Where scupper'd, and to DUP in thrall,
  She fails to direct Brexit processes.
  O England! model to thy inward thinking,
  Like perfidious Albion on speed,
  What mightst May do, that honour would thee do,
  Were all thy Tabloids kind and natural!
  But see thy fault! Tusk hath in thee found out
  A nest of hollow bosoms, which he fills
  With treacherous crowns; and three corrupted men,
  One, Kenneth Clarke of Rushcliffe, and the second,

Rory Stewart of Penrith, and the third,
Sir David Gauke, knight of Hertfordshire,
Have, for the gilt of France, – O guilt indeed! –
Confirm'd conspiracy with the EU;
And by their hands Mrs May must fail,
For the ERG hold her feet to fire,
Ere they take shit from these Europeans.
Linger your patience on, and we'll digest
The abuse of distance, force a play.
The sum is paid; the traitors are agreed;
Barnier's taunts reach London; and the scene
Is now transported, gentles, to Westminster.
There is the playhouse now, there must you sit;
And Brussels thence shall we convey you safe,
And bring you back, charming the narrow seas
To give you gentle pass; for, if we may,
We'll not offend one stomach with our play.
But, till Ma May comes forth, and not till then,
Unto Westminster do we shift our scene.

SCENE I

Westminster Hall.
The Commons below. Enter JOHN BERCOW, MARK FRANCOIS,
DESMOND SWAYNE, STEVE BAKER, ANNA SOUBRY, KEN
CLARKE, AMBER RUDD, RORY STEWART, GAVIN WILLIAMSON
and attendants.

JOHN BERCOW
    Call forth Hammond.
                    Enter WHIPS *with* PHILIP HAMMOND.

Now, Hammond, freely speak thy mind,
What thou dost know of May's third exit deal,
Who wrought it with such ease, and who perform'd
The bloody office of its timeless end.

PHILIP HAMMOND

Then set before my face the ERG.

JOHN BERCOW

Now, Tories, stand forth, and look on these men.

PHILIP HAMMOND

Mark Francois, I know your daredevil tongue
Does scorn to unsay what once it delivered.
In that dead time when the bill's death was planned,
I heard you say, 'Is not my arm of length,
That reacheth from my Essex cul-de-sac
As far as Windsor, to mine PM's head?'
Amongst much other talk that very time
I heard you say that you had loth refuse
'The offer of an hundred thousand Frubes,
Than Baker's Spartans rubber stamp this deal',
Adding withal, how blest this land would be
When 'Brexit means Brexit'.

MARK FRANCOIS

Tories and Lords,
What answer shall I make to this base man?
My father, Reginald Francois, was a
D-Day veteran. He to bullying
By any Germans never submitted
And nor will his son: Mark ne Francois pas.
Shall I dishonour my fair Essex stars
On equal terms to give him chastisement?
Either I must, or have mine honour soiled
By this wretched Airbus apologist.

    There is my gage, the manual seal of death
    That marks thee out for hell. I say thou liest,
    And will maintain that what I said is this:
    'I'm Mark Francois. I wasn't trained to lose.'

JOHN BERCOW
    Phil, forbear. Do not pick up his paintball glove.

MARK FRANCOIS
    O Spreadsheet Philip, would he were the best
    In all this presence that hath moved me so.

KEN CLARKE
If that thy valour stand on sympathy there is my string-backed leather driving glove, Penfold, in gage to thine. By those Pepp'rami wrappers where thou stand'st, I heard thee say, and vauntingly thou spak'st, that thou would cause One Nationism's death, if thou deniest it twenty times, thou liest! And I will turn thy falsehood to thy arse, where it was forged, with this suede Hush Puppy.

MARK FRANCOIS
    Thou dar'st not, coward, live to see that day.

KEN CLARKE
    Oh now, by my plump soul, I would it were this hour.

STEVE BAKER
    Kenneth, thou liest. Mark's honour is as true
    In this appeal as thou art all refined;
    TAs aren't trained to lose, and I throw mine,
    To prove it on thee to the extremest point
    Of mortal breathing. Seize it if thou dar'st.

KEN CLARKE
And if I do not, may my hands rot off, and tarnish ever more the noble name of British American Tobacco.

AMBER RUDD
    I task the earth to the like, forsworn Steve,

Spare me thy jingoistic macho crap
You one-pint-Rambo, shit Les Dennis, for
As May is hamstrung by thy treacherous plots,
From sun to sun, there is my honour's pawn.
Engage it to the trial if thou dar'st.
STEVE BAKER
Rudd sets us too! By Windrush, I'll throw at all.
I have a thousand spirits in one breast
For I am Brexit Hardman Steve Baker.
RORY STEWART
My Lord Baker, I do remember well
The very time Francois and you did talk.
STEVE BAKER
'Tis very true. You were in presence then,
So you can witness th'Airbus Wars are true.
RORY STEWART
As false, by heaven, as heaven itself is true.
STEVE BAKER
Stewart, thou liest.
RORY STEWART
Dishonourable Steve!
In proof whereof, there is my honour's pawn.
Pick it up, or else on my podcast guest.
STEVE BAKER
Typical. A Karl Lagerfeld fur glove.
How fondly dost thou spur the German horse!
If I dare eat, or drink, or breathe, or live,
I dare meet Stewart in a lorry park,
And spit upon him, whilst I say he lies,
And lies, and lies. Here is my bond of faith:
No deal is better than a bad deal. Ha!
Besides, I heard Airbus' CEO say

That thou, Stewart, didst send two of thy men
To infiltrate an ERG foam party.
DESMOND SWAYNE
Some honest Christian trust me with a gage.
This Stewart spies! Here do I throw my sock,
If he may be compelled to try his honour.
MARK FRANCOIS
Stay out of this, Des. This is big boy shit.
Enter GRAHAM BRADY.
GRAHAM BRADY
That inglorious day may soon be seen.
Many a time hath Theresa May run
For Anglican thrills, through vast fields of wheat,
Streaming the ensign 'Hostile 'vironment'
'Gainst Albanians, Poles, Turks, refugees.
Yet, toiled with failed withdrawal has just quit
To irrelevance, on back benches green,
Returning to bland triviality,
And her pure soul unto its captain, Phil,
Under whose colours she has failed so long.
JOHN BERCOW
Why, Brady, has May resigned?
GRAHAM BRADY
As surely as I live, my lord.
GAVIN WILLIAMSON
Sweet peace conduct her failed deal to Ted Heath's
Warm bosom. Tories, appellants, hear this:
Your differences shall all rest under gage
Till we confirm I'm getting made a Sir.
Enter NADINE DORRIES, unattended.

NADINE DORRIES
　　Great Conservatives, I, Nads, come to thee
　　From Boris himself, who with willing soul
　　Does approve himself next Prime Minister,
　　Natural leader of our British lands.
　　Let's support his claim, ignore his flaws and
　　Make Boris PM, of that name the first!
AMBER RUDD
　　In God's name, no. Defend us from this oaf.
　　　　　　　　　　　　　　Enter MAX HASTINGS.
GAVIN WILLIAMSON
　　Max Hastings? What are you now doing here?
MAX HASTINGS
　　Idiot. Silence.
　　Worst in this loyal presence may I speak,
　　Yet best beseeming me to speak the truth.
　　Make Boris PM? O, God forfend it,
　　That in a climate Conservative, you
　　Should do so heinous, black, obscene a deed!
　　I speak to Tories, an ex-Tory speaks,
　　Stirred up by God, Pitt, Peel, Heath and Thatcher
　　The right hon member for Uxbridge, de Pfeff,
　　Is a foul traitor to Conservatism.
　　And if you crown him, let me prophesy
　　The blood of pensioners'll manure the ground
　　And future ages groan for this foul act.
　　Your guilt will reign as he piles bodies high,
　　And in this seat of peace needless Brexit strife
　　Shall kin with kin and kind with kind confound.
　　Disorder, chaos, fear and fiasco

  Shall here inhabit, and this land be called
  The field of Golgotha and dead men's skulls.
  O, if you raise this Clown inside this House,
  It will the woefullest division prove
  That ever fell upon this Brexter'd earth.
  Prevent it, resist it, let it not be so,
  Lest child, child's children, cry against you, 'NO!'

NADINE DORRIES
  Well have you argued, Max; and, for your pains,
  Of capital treason I arrest you.
  My Lords of ERG, be it your charge
  To keep him safely till his day of trial.

DESMOND SWAYNE
  Max Hastings, you are in my custody,
  Procure your sureties for your trial day.
  Your bail, at two fat pigeons, shall be set.
  Little are we beholding to your love,
  You traitorous hawker of sovereignty.

NADINE DORRIES
  I will tell May, so that in common view,
  We can move straight to Boris's anointing.

MARK FRANCOIS
  Her conduct I will be. I wasn't trained to lose.

          Cheering. Exeunt.

SCENE II

Enter THERESA MAY, *sad, led by* PHILIP MAY.

PHILIP MAY
  How does Fluffy?

THERESA MAY
>O Puffy, sick to death.
>My legs like loaden branches bow to th' earth,
>Willing to leave their burden. Reach a chair. *She sits.*
>So. Now, methinks, I feel a little ease.
>Didst thou not tell me, Puffy, as thou made tea,
>That my life's work, the third withdrawal bill,
>Was dead?

PHILIP MAY
>Yes, Fluffy, but I thought Fluffy,
>Out of the stress she suffered, gave no ear to't.

THERESA MAY
>Prithee, good Puffy, tell me how it died.
>If well, it stepped before my vocation
>For my example.

PHILIP MAY
>Well, the voice goes, madam.
>For after the stout Andrea Leadsom
>Resignèd as your Leader of the House,
>In protest at your withdrawal strategy.
>It fell sick suddenly and grew so ill
>It could not pass the House.

THERESA MAY
>Alas, poor bill!

PHILIP MAY
>At last, with raucous Brexiteers outside,
>Lodged by the Houses, drinking lager beer,
>And our honourable members within;
>You finally united Parliament:
>With MPs from all sides opposing it.
>It went to lay its weary bones midst them.

Give it a little earth for charity
Is the best thing we can do for it now.

THERESA MAY
 So may it rest. I'faith it could ne'er pass,
 T'was more compromised than Boris with a
 Skins-party hangover from Evgeny's.
 Yet thus far, Puffy, give me leave to speak:
 Its promises were, as it then was, poor;
 But its performance, as it is now, nothing.
 By mine own Party I am beat, and give
 The future ill example.

PHILIP MAY
 Noble Fluffy,
 Our evil manners live in brass; our virtues
 We write in water. May it please my Fluffy
 To hear me speak your good now?

THERESA MAY
 Yes please, Puffy;
 I were malicious else.

PHILIP MAY
 This Fluffy,
 Though from an humble stock, undoubtedly
 Was fashioned to much honour. From her cradle
 She was a scholar, and a ripe and good one,
 Exceeding stern, harsh-spoken, and with red lines;
 Sour, lofty, grave to those that loved her not,
 But to that man that sought her, sweet as summer.
 'Twixt stalks of wheat or polyester sheets,
 Her Puffy never unsatisfied was.
 So forget her endless 'meaningful votes'.
 Unwilling to outlive the good that did it;

Since, though her career is finishèd now –
Obdurance. Weakness. She did live her brand,
And Anglicans shall ever speak these virtues.
This overthrow heaps happiness upon her,
She can at last go on a Saga cruise,
And find the blessedness of being little.
And, to add greater honours to her age
At least she failed, fearing almighty God.

THERESA MAY
After I fail, I wish no other herald,
No other speaker of my living actions,
To keep mine honour from corruption
But such unbiased chronicler as Puffy.
Cause the musicians play me 'Dancing Queen'
My walk-on, whilst I sit meditating
On Brexit's poor show which I now escape.
                    Music: Abba's 'Dancing Queen'.

PHILIP MAY
She is asleep. Good wench, I'll sit down quiet,
For fear I wake her. Softly, gentle Fluffy.   *The vision:
Enter, solemnly tripping one after another, Agnetha, Benny,
Björn and Frida, clad in white robes, wearing on their heads
garlands of wheat, with masks made of golden export licences,
twirling red tapes in their hands. They first congee, then dance
through fields of wheat, at certain changes, the first holds a
withdrawal bill over their head, at which they tear it up while
the other three make reverent curtsies. They each repeat the
process. At which, as it were by inspiration, she makes in her sleep
signs of rejoicing and holdeth up her hands to heaven. And so in
their dancing, vanish, into Sunlit Uplands.
                    The music continues.*

THERESA MAY
  Social democratic Swedes? Are ye gone?
  And leave me in wretchedness behind ye?
PHILIP MAY
  Fluffy, I am here.
THERESA MAY
  It is not you I call for.
  Saw ye none enter since I slept?
PHILIP MAY
  None, Fluffy.
THERESA MAY
  No? Saw you not this combo power pop
  Invite me to a wheat field, whose bright faces
  Cast thousand beams upon me, like the sun?
  They promised me eternal happiness
  And brought spelt garlands, Puppy. Gluten wreaths
  I am not worthy yet to wear. I shall, assuredly.
PHILIP MAY
  Spelt?
THERESA MAY
  S P E L T
PHILIP MAY
  No, I, er, nevermind. I'm joyful, ma'am,
  Glad that such good dreams possess your fancy.
THERESA MAY
  Bid the music leave,
  Lest into robot dancing I do break.
            Music ceases. Enter GAVIN WILLIAMSON.
GAVIN WILLIAMSON
  An't like your ex-Grace –

THERESA MAY
>You're a saucy shit.
>Deserve we no more reverence?

PHILIP MAY
>You are to blame, Uriah Heep, failed whip
>You snivelling hawker of fireplaces,
>To use so rude behaviour. Go to, kneel.

GAVIN WILLIAMSON
>I humbly entreat your Highness's pardon.
>Haste made me unmannerly. There is a
>Simpleton sent from Boris to see you.

THERESA MAY
>Admit them entrance, Puffy. But this fellow
>Let me ne'er see again.   *Exit GAVIN WILLIAMSON.*
>   *Enter NADINE DORRIES.*
>If my sight fail not,
>You should be the clogs and shawls romance scribe,
>Boris's scythe he uses to crack nuts,
>Your name Nadine Dorries.

NADINE DORRIES
>Yes, ma'am, the same.

THERESA MAY
>O my lord,
>The times and titles now are altered strangely
>With me since first you knew me. But I pray you,
>What is your pleasure with me?

NADINE DORRIES
>Failed PM,
>First, mine own service to your Grace; the next,
>Boris requests that I would visit you,

Who grieves much for your weakness, and by me
He sends you his princely commendations,
And thanks. For opening the door for him.
THERESA MAY
O good lord, that comfort comes not at all;
'Tis like execution after a pardon.
But now I am past all comforts here but prayers.
How does this Johnson?
NADINE DORRIES
Madam, in rude health.
THERESA MAY
So will these Etonians ever be,
While I shall dwell with worms, and my poor name
Banish'd the kingdom. Puffy, is that note
I caused you write yet sent away?
PHILIP MAY
No, Fluffy. *Giving it to her.*
THERESA MAY
Nads, I do humbly pray you to give this
To he you stalk with telephoto lens.
NADINE DORRIES
Most willing, madam.
THERESA MAY
In which I've commended his unfitness
The model of sloth. His mean acolytes
More than one can count, drool thick around him
Beseeching him to deliver Brexit,
From single markets, customs unions,
By deadline of October thirty-first.
To Europe Leave, for leaving's own damned sake,
The OBR knows how costly. My next,
I hope the lazy git has notion vague

How a hard Irish border might start to
Unravel the delicate Stormont peace.
Of which there is not one, I dare do avow
And now I should not lie – but will deserve,
If the Good Friday Agreement does fail,
Together with those plastic patriots,
Cash, Hannan, Redwood, Baker, Bone; the scorn
Of Hell and of Derry (Londonderry).
The last is, for all our sakes, stop the lies.
His deceits are prolific and well known
Bar unto the saps that he has sold 'em,
This something I ask he remember me by.
If Brady had pleased to give longer reign
And less internal strife, we'd not part thus.
These are the contents, and, my Nadine, good,
By that you love the dearest in this world,
AKA Boris, honour he you stalk,
Stand you your constituents' friend, and urge
Him, do me this last right.

NADINE DORRIES
  Have you quite finishèd?
  I won't hear a bad word said against him.

THERESA MAY
  Then go, you silly wench. Remember me
  In all humility unto his pomp.
  For his long trouble now is passing on.
  He is World King. Tell him I did curse him,
  For so I will. Farewell. Mine career dims,
  Oh, Phil. Puffy, get the Saga brochure.
  The Garden Centres and Carveries call
  Let's road trip! Repurpose a 'Go Home' van
  And sally forth on a National Trust tour

Of stately homes and Roman forts with not
A vegan scone or slaver's guilt in sight.
We always ourselves promisèd we would.
Get a road map. No longer PM she
A queen to Puffy, Fluffy shall well be.
To the A1(M). *Exeunt.*

SCENE III

A public place near Westminster Abbey.
Enter YOUNG TORIES, *strewing rushes.*

FIRST YOUNG TORY
More champers, more champers.

SECOND YOUNG TORY
The trumpets have sounded twice.

FIRST YOUNG TORY
'Twill be two o'clock ere they come from the coronation.
Dispatch, dispatch.

White smoke comes from the chimney of Westminster.

SECOND YOUNG TORY
Fumata bianca! We have a new leader. *Exeunt.*
Trumpets sound, and BORIS JOHNSON *and his train pass over the stage. Enter* KEN CLARKE, NICHOLAS SOAMES, DAVID GAUKE *and* RORY STEWART.

KEN CLARKE
Stand here by me, Master Rory Stewart. I will make Boris do us grace. I will leer upon him as he comes by and do but mark the countenance that he will give me.

RORY STEWART
God bless thy cigar-filled lungs, noble Ken.
KEN CLARKE
Come here, Nick Soames, stand behind me.
NICHOLAS SOAMES
I will thy noble liver inflame, Ken
And make thee rage, they're saying Boris plans
To remove the whip, and to expel us,
A plan the coward will execute with
Mark Spencer's mechanical, dirty hand.
Rouse revenge and stub out your Café Crème,
For he makes moves. Nick Soames speaks nought but truth.
KEN CLARKE
O, but I wouldn't have bestowed the thousand pounds I borrowed of you on the San Marino grand prix if this was true. But tis no matter. I'll wager you it, or 5 per cent of our GDP, whichever the larger, that I can fix this. This doth imply the zeal I have to see the silly pup, who I will now induce to deliver, for his elders, a sensible Brexit.
RORY STEWART
Ken, I'm not entirely sure that it doth.
KEN CLARKE
It shows too that my earnestness of affection for him is kin to that I have for jazz –
RORY STEWART
I am not convinced of this either, Ken.
KEN CLARKE
My devotion to cigars, my affinity with pints –
RORY STEWART
Ken. Boris has not one care in the world.
He would drop us as quickly as he would

His boxer shorts 'pon sight of a charmed aide.

KEN CLARKE
As it were, I did take the Tube from watching a matinee of Verdi's *Falstaff* at Covent Garden, and did not deliberate with a scotch, but came straight here –

RORY STEWART
I don't think, Ken, that is as amusing
As I think you think mentioning it sounds.

KEN CLARKE
And standing here, stained with nicotine, sweating Theakston, thinking of nothing else, as if there were nothing else to be done but let him know, 'Here I am, putting all affairs else in oblivion, until we reverse this Brexit'.

NICHOLAS SOAMES
'Tis *semper idem*, for *obsque hoc nihil est*; 'tis all in every part.

KEN CLARKE
Faith. I will deliver us. *Shouts within. The kazoos sound.*

NICHOLAS SOAMES
There roar'd the sea, and trumpet-clangor sounds.

Enter BORIS JOHNSON, MARK SPENCER, PRITI PATEL, DOMINIC RAAB, LIZ TRUSS *and* MATT HANCOCK.

KEN CLARKE
Johnson, de Pfeff, Boris.

NICHOLAS SOAMES
The heavens keep thee (incompetent imp)!

RORY STEWART
God save thee, metastatic chancer, hail.

BORIS JOHNSON
Mark Spencer, promptly speak to those vain men.

MARK SPENCER
  Have you your wits? Know you what 'tis you speak?
KEN CLARKE
My King! My Jove! I speak to thee, my heart!
MARK SPENCER
  Are you being sarcastic?
KEN CLARKE
Yes.
BORIS JOHNSON
  I know thee not, old man. Fall to thy knees.
  Lord, how ill white hair becomes yellow stains.
  I have long dreamt of such a kind of man,
  So surfeit-swell'd, so old, so saluted;
  But, being awaked, I do deride him.
  Make less thy body hence, and more thy grace;
  Leave gormandizing; know the grave doth gape
  For thee thrice wider than for other men.
KEN CLARKE
Are you talking about yourself?
BORIS JOHNSON
  Reply not to me with a fool-born jest.
  Presume not that I am the thing I was;
  For Uxbridge doth know, so shall the world see,
  That BoJo's away turn'd from sex and lies;
  And I will now get mighty Brexit done.
  When thou dost hear that I have failed in this,
  Approach me, and thou shalt be as thou wast,
  The grandee who did never quite make it.
  Till then I banish thee, on pain of death,
  As I do the rest of the Remainers,
  Not to come near Westminster by ten mile.

For competence of life I'll allow you,
Grudgingly, to go on *Politics Live*
And Sky News. As you do reform yourselves,
We might, according to your depth of flattery,
Give advancement to the Lords. I charge you,
To see perform'd the tenor of our word.
  Set on.   *Exeunt* JOHNSON *with his train.*

KEN CLARKE
Mr Soames, I owe you 5 per cent of our GDP.

NICHOLAS SOAMES
  Yea, marry, Ken Clarke. I would prefer my
  Three thousand pounds. Which I beseech you let
  Me have back with me to my Fletching home.

KEN CLARKE
That can hardly be, Soamesy. Do not you grieve at this; I
  shall send for him in private. He cannot just overturn the
  old order without care for precedent. Look you, he must
  seem thus to the world. Fear not your advancements; I
  will be the man yet that shall pierce his vacuous
  pomposity.

NICHOLAS SOAMES
  I cannot perceive how? He cares for order not.
  And procedure? He's a moral bankrupt, Ken,
  'Tis rooted in his contempt for the truth.
  I beseech you, let me have one of my
  Three K. My speeding fines won't themselves pay.

KEN CLARKE
Sir, I will be as good as my word. Jack shall woo Jill, naught
  shall go ill. This that you heard was but a mood.

RORY STEWART
  Or a mound. That I fear he shall die on.

KEN CLARKE
Fear no mounds. Go with me to the Garrick. Come,
Nicholas Soames; come, Rory Stewart. I'll send for him
soon at night.
>*Enter* MARK SPENCER, PRITI PATEL, DOMINIC RAAB,
>LIZ TRUSS *and* MATT HANCOCK, OFFICERS
>*with them.*

MARK SPENCER
Go, carry Kenneth Clarke to Belmarsh nick.
Take all his company along with him.
KEN CLARKE
My lord, my lord.
MARK SPENCER
I cannot now speak. Remove them the whip.
They're traitors, do not listen to their lies.
NICHOLAS SOAMES
Si fortuna me tormenta, spero me contenta.
>*Exeunt all but* PATEL, RAAB, TRUSS *and* HANCOCK.

PRITI PATEL
I like this fair proceeding of de Pfeff's.
His intent that these Euro wallowers
Shall all be deposed, means thus, Brexit thrives,
And all are banish'd till their dialogues
More wise and modest appear. Like ours are.
DOMINIC RAAB
Did you know that the UK relies on
The Dover Calais strait for lots of trade?
PRITI PATEL
No? Really? Boris hath call'd Cabinet.
DOMINIC RAAB
And Priti, Matt, Liz and Dom are in it.

PRITI PATEL
  It's a brave new dawn.
MATT HANCOCK
  There's an important question here. Who's Dawn?
LIZ TRUSS
  My handbag is full of twigs.
PRITI PATEL
  Ere this year expire, I will lay odds that,
  We'll bear our civil swords and native fire
  For Brexit clean. I heard a bird so sing,
  Whose music I stopped with sharp kitten heel.
  Come, will you hence?   *Exeunt.*

SCENE IV

The BBC.
Enter LAURA KUENSSBERG and NIGEL FARAGE.

LAURA KUENSSBERG
  I'm with the affable nativist and,
  By his school teachers' account, racist true,
  Nige Farage, architect of Brexit's coup.
NIGEL FARAGE
  Good morning, Laura. Thanks for having me.
LAURA KUENSSBERG
  Fair morning to thee, balance-giving Nige.
NIGEL FARAGE
  God and his angels guard your splendid show
  And make you long become it.
LAURA KUENSSBERG
  Thank you for so saying. I would be keen

To hear much from you, nuance provider,
Concerning our failed Brexit withdrawal.
And God forbid, my dear and faithful guest,
That you should fashion, wrest or cow your views,
Or nicely charge your hatred-riddled soul.

NIGEL FARAGE
Then hear me, gracious Laura, viewers too,
The cause of Brexit verges history.
Else Turks will flood from Dungeness to Rhyl.

LAURA KUENSSBERG
My learnèd Nige, we pray you to say more
And justly and race-baitingly tell us
Why the votes you nick make the Tories dance
A mothlike jig, straight to Farage's flames?

NIGEL FARAGE
Of course I will, balancèd Laura K.
For in *The Art of the Deal* it is writ,
'When virtue dies, let its legacy then
Fall into the lap of the grifter.' Scribe,
I stand for Britain! Let's go WTO!
Or else in bondage to Van Rompuy stay.
Our biggest tyranny is status quo.
We're Saxons; unleash Offa's zeal, and like
The Hammer of the Frogs, strong Mrs T,
Who at Fontainebleau did our rebate win,
Defeating Europe's superpower sound,
Whiles her most milklorn children here at home
Watched in awe, beaming at brave Friedman's whelp.

LAURA KUENSSBERG
May's withdrawal deal fell short.
Do we now expect you will rouse your men?

NIGEL FARAGE
  So, let our courage follow, Miss Kuenssberg,
  With referendum we have won the Right
  To withdraw. We polled patriotically.
  Now insurrection and chaos threaten
  For never content will Brexiteers be
  'Til ourselves, we impose sanctions on.

LAURA KUENSSBERG
  What of free trade?

NIGEL FARAGE
  Let them eat sovereignty.

LAURA KUENSSBERG
  You really shoot from the hip don't you, Nige.
  But if the eagle England goes her own way,
  Might not then the Scots and Welsh elope too?

NIGEL FARAGE
  Thus, Brexit doth perpetually rend,
  In divers schisms, discords, strifes, and leagues,
  In constant motion setting: upheaval
  To which is fixèd, as an aim or butt,
  Sovereignty; for so work the honey-bees,
  Creatures that by a rule in nature teach
  The act of order to a sovereign realm.
  They've a PM and ministers of sorts,
  Some, like Brexiteers, trade on nostalgia,
  Others, like merchants, must not trade abroad,
  Others, in hedges, armèd in their stings,
  Make boot upon the shorting of the pound,
  Which pillage they with merry march send 'home'
  To offshore havens, while, non-domiciled
  And busied in their luxury, look on

The singing masons building uplands gold,
The foodbank citizens for honey queue
The poor mechanic porters crowding in
The harried trawlerman at barren port,
And sad-eyed justice, with his surly hum,
Delivering to executors pale
The lazy Remain drone.

LAURA KUENSSBERG
And what would you say to your detractors?

NIGEL FARAGE
We won our Brexit without a shot fired.
We've taken control back, Britannia's free,
And just like Dresden, Europe again fears
Our Bomber Command of Tice, Wigmore, Banks.
If we, with thrice such power brought back home,
Cannot defend our own doors from the dogs,
Let us be worried and our nation lose
Its name of John Bullheaded doggedness.

LAURA KUENSSBERG
For your time, Nigel, dearly I thank you.
Now, Carol Kirkwood's got the latest weather.

SCENE V

Enter BORIS JOHNSON, DOMINIC CUMMINGS *and* DAVID FROST.

BORIS JOHNSON
Call in the messengers from von der Ley'n.
                    Exeunt some ATTENDANTS.
Now BoJo's resolv'd; and with Dom Raab's guile,

Dom Cumming's laser pen, Frost's charisma
And Barclay's Filofax, I'll get us out,
I'll bend them to my Oven Ready deal.
I'll sit, either ruling from Bude to Leeds,
Or Europe and her Federalist dukedoms,
Will lay these moobs in an unworthy urn
Tombless, with no wunderbra over them.
                Enter faceless European BUREAUCRATS.
Now am I prepar'd to lay down the law
With our fair cousin Ursula. We hear
Your greeting is from her, let's hear you sing.

FIRST BUREAUCRAT
May't please your Majesty to give us leave
Freely to render what we have in charge,
Or shall we sparingly show you far off
Der Leyen's meaning and our embassy?

BORIS JOHNSON
BoJo's no tyrant, therefore with frank
Uncurbèd plainness speak der Leyen's mind.

FIRST BUREAUCRAT
Thus, then, in few.
Your Highness, lately sending unto us
To claim some special status, ungranted
To your weak predecessor, Theresa,
In answer of which, Europe speaks as one:
And says you savour too much your own hype,
And bids you be advis'd that David Frost's
Negotiating skills could not from us
Win toffee, never mind new concessions.
She therefore sends you balm for your sad soul,

This tun of treasure; and, in lieu of this,
Asks that you let the status that you claim
Hear no more of you. Ursula this speaks.
BORIS JOHNSON
What treasure, Cummings? *CUMMINGS opens the box.*
DOMINIC CUMMINGS
Nissan parts, my liege.
BORIS JOHNSON
We are glad der Leyen is such a drollster, yet
Her jest will savour but of shallow wit,
When Europhiles, into their pilsners blub.
Convey them with safe conduct. Fare you well.
Exeunt BUREAUCRATS.
DOMINIC CUMMINGS
An illogical communication.
BORIS JOHNSON
We hope to make the sender blush at it.
BORIS JOHNSON
OK, Frosty, omit no happy hour
That may give prep to your deal-making team;
For we have now no thought in us but this:
The Irish backstop business is our key.
Onwards! Let our proportions for this war
Of words be collected. And mark my words:
'No border we'll see in the Irish sea.'
March we with passports blue, thrusting before,
Or I'll hide Johnson behind Smeg fridge door.
Therefore let every man now task his thought,
Whilst I do prorogue, and see this deal bought.
Exeunt JOHNSON and FROST.

SCENE VI

Brussels.
Enter URSULA VON DER LEYEN, JEAN-CLAUDE JUNCKER,
MICHEL BARNIER, ANGELA MERKEL, THERESA MAY,
FRANÇOIS HOLLANDE, DONALD TUSK.

FRANÇOIS HOLLANDE
David Frost! O *diable*!
MICHEL BARNIER
O *Seigneur*! *le jour est perdu, tout est perdu*!
URSULA VON DER LEYEN
Alles ist verwirrend, alles!
Tapferer Boris, tapferes Britannien!
They've comprehensively outwitted us.
They'll end legally, frictionless free trade,
Pay alimony, forty billion,
And put a border in the Irish Sea.
Shame, disgrace and reproach everlasting
Sits mocking in our self-satisfied plumes.

A short alarum.

O *mechante* fortune! Do not run away.
MICHEL BARNIER
Why, all our ranks are broke.
JEAN-CLAUDE JUNCKER
O perdurable shame! Let's sack ourselves.
And scuttle the European project.
Be this the David Frost we play'd dice for?
MICHEL BARNIER
Or the same unfaithful Prime Minister
Who's had more kids than I've had *haute* dinners?

DONALD TUSK
    We have been by Albion outflankèd.
    They never from the table took 'no deal'
    Which means we must continue to trade free
    Whiles upon themselves, they self-sanctions place.
    Let us go hence and, with our caps in hand
    Like debased panders, hold the BA door
    For ace negotiator, David Frost.

ANGELA MERKEL
    Overconfidence hath spoil'd us. The spoils
    Claim our vanquishers: roaming charges, queues,
    And hoovers over fourteen hundred watts.

URSULA VON DER LEYEN
    Then let our last act of suave petulance
    Be to choke the Inselaffe on red tape.

DONALD TUSK
    Give what they want? A crude federal trick!
    And robust response to their inane schtick. *Exeunt.*

SCENE VII

Westminster, 19 October.
Enter DOMINIC CUMMINGS, MICHAEL
GOVE, PRITI PATEL, ANDREA LEADSOM,
DOMINIC RAAB, MARK FRANCOIS, STEVE BAKER,
KWASI KWARTENG.

MICHAEL GOVE
    Not since the Falklands War of eighty-two
    Has Parliament on a Saturday met.

MARK FRANCOIS
  Port Stanley. I remember it too well.
ANDREA LEADSOM
  Mark Francois, don't be so ridiculous.
MARK FRANCOIS
  The saucy Paras stole the glory ours.
  But TA Catering were the first boots down.
DOMINIC CUMMINGS
  No, Francois. Silence. Boris, where is he?
KWASI KWARTENG
  He's flying back from Brussels as we speak,
  With oven-ready deal to sell the floor.
DOMINIC RAAB
  He's secured the Will of the People in
  A metaphor that on their level works:
  A ghastly disposable ready meal.
DOMINIC CUMMINGS
  Our estate trash need no compelling. It's
  Retrograde legislators who need their
  Heads knocking together: the Tories, Libs,
  SNP, Labour. Soubry, Clarke and Soames.
STEVE BAKER
  God's arm strike with us! 'tis a fearful odds.
  Like Spartans we must present ourselves firm;
  I will tell the rest of the ERG.
  If we no more meet till Elysium –
  From Wycombe High to Thermopylae I.
DOMINIC RAAB
  Farewell, bespectacled evangelist;
  And yet I do thee wrong to mind thee of it,
  For thou art well framèd, when wearing naught
  But your loin cloth, and Spartan gospel truth.

MARK FRANCOIS
  Go well, brave Baker; or should I now say
  Brave Leonidas?
STEVE BAKER
  Tis all one to this adrenaline fiend.
  Sky diving, motorcycling and, of course,
  Fast catamaran sailing make him tick.
  Nobody sees through this white-knuckle shtick.
                              Exit BAKER.
ANDREA LEADSOM
  He's as full of valour as charisma;
  This Beaconsfield Boudicca, big in both.
                        Enter BORIS JOHNSON.
PRITI PATEL
  O that the whips had more
  Dirt to dish on those rivals in Remain
  That will not vote to-day!
BORIS JOHNSON
  What's she that wishes so?
  Young Pritster Patel? No, my fair harpy;
  If we are mark'd to win, we must deceive
  To bring our country out; For us to Leave,
  The more we lie, the greater chance of triumph.
  God's will I pray thee hear my breaking news:
  By Gove, we have done a world-beating deal.
  What care I whose export businesses fail?
  It yearns me not if the M20 halts;
  Such tiresome things dwell not in my concerns.
  For if it be a sin to covet freedom,
  I am the most offending soul alive.
  Yes. Oven Ready the deal is! Faith, dudes,
  Hail, Frosty! I'd lief lose lessons of IT

Than Parliament reject this ready meal.
It's the best hope we have. You could not wish for
 more!
Rather proclaim it, dear Pritster, to the House,
That he, which has no stomach for this fight,
Let Doubters, Doomsters, Gloomsters depart now.
In democracy I will restore trust;
I would not lie in that man's company
That rates not Sovereignty, to lie with us.
This day is call'd the feast of Crispian.
He that sustains Odey, and comes safe home,
Will stand a tip-toe when this day is nam'd,
And rouse him at the thought of Asset Funds.
He that shall live this day, and see old age,
Will yearly on the vigil feast his neighbours,
And say 'To-morrow is Saint Crispian.'
Then will he strip his sleeve and show his watch,
And say 'This Rolex got I from Odey.'
Old men forget; yet all shall be forgot,
But he'll remember, with advantages,
Which vote he cast that day. Then shall our fame,
Familiar in his mouth as household names –
Boris and Farage, Dacre, William Cash,
Chope, Cummings, Corbyn, and Mark ne-Francois-
 pas –
Be in their flowing cups freshly rememb'red.
This story shall the teacher teach his charge;
And Crispin Crispian shall ne'er go by,
From this day to the ending of the world,
But we in it shall be remembered –

We few, we happy few, we gang of grifters;
For he to-day that votes to leave with me
Shall be my grifter; be he ne'er so vile,
This day shall improve his condition;
And layabouts in England now-a-bed
Shall think themselves accurs'd they were not here,
And hold their futures cheap whiles any speaks
Than hedged with us upon Saint Odey's day.

DOMINC RAAB
For sovereignty, bestow yourself with speed:
For Remain bravely in their lobby sit,
And will with borders frictionless charge us.

BORIS JOHNSON
All things are ready, if our minds be so.

PRITI PATEL
Perish the man whose mind is backward now!

MARK FRANCOIS
Why, then, did you all just look upon me?

PRITI PATEL
Oh, Francois! Mark! Would you and I alone,
Without more help, could fight this royal battle!

BORIS JOHNSON
You know your places:
Cry 'God for Boris, England and Saint George.'

Exeunt.

JOHN BERCOW
The ayes to the right three hundred and fifty-eight, the noes to the left two hundred and thirty-four. The ayes have it. The ayes have it. *Shouting.*

SCENE VIII

A room in a Wetherspoons.
Enter JONATHAN GULLIS, LEE ANDERSON, MIRIAM CATES,
NICK FLETCHER, BRENDAN CLARKE-SMITH, MARK
JENKINSON *and* ANDREA JENKYNS.

MIRIAM CATES
Is all our company here?

LEE ANDERSON
A up. You were best to call them generally, man by man, according to the candidate list.

MIRIAM CATES
Here is the scroll of every Tory's name, which is thought fit through all northern Britain, to smash the Red Wall, ahead of the election day at night.

LEE ANDERSON
First, good Miriam Cates, say what the initiative treats on; then read the names of the candidates; and so grow to a point.

MIRIAM CATES
Marry, our platform is The Most Wonderful Delivery of a Brexit Deal Oven Ready and The Most Cruel Death of Labour in Its Own Heartlands.

LEE ANDERSON
A very good piece of work, I assure you. Because I'm in it. Now, good Miriam Cates, call forth our candidates by the scroll. Masters, spread yourselves.

MIRIAM CATES
Answer, as I call you. Lee Anderson, the miner.

ACT II, SCENE VIII | 81

LEE ANDERSON
Ready. Name what part I am for and proceed.
MIRIAM CATES
You, Lee Anderson, are set down for Ashfield firebrand.
LEE ANDERSON
What is an Ashfield firebrand – a fluffer, or a tyrant?
MIRIAM CATES
A fluffer, that agitates most gallantly, to tell foreigners to 'fuck off back to France'.
LEE ANDERSON
That will ask some tears in the true performing of it. If I do it, let the audience look to their pies. I will move storms; I will condole in some measure. To the rest – yet my chief humour is for a tyrant. I could play Enoch Powell rarely, or a part to play the twat in, to make all split.

The raging schlock
Of gibbering cocks
Shall put a block
On immigrants,
And benefits Tsars
Shall reach from far,
And stop and bar
False fake claimants.

This was lofty. Now name the rest of the players. This is Donald Trump's vein, a tyrant's vein; a fluffer is more condoling.
MIRIAM CATES
Jonathan Gullis, the PG Tips advert extra.
JONATHAN GULLIS
Here, Miriam Cates.

MIRIAM CATES
Gullis, you must take gender dysphoria on you in Stoke-on-Trent, Kidsgrove and Talke.
JONATHAN GULLIS
Nay, faith, let not me be a woman. I have a beard coming.
MIRIAM CATES
No, Jonathan. It is an ideology that we must loathe.
JONATHAN GULLIS
I don't know anything about it, yet I already loathe it.
LEE ANDERSON
And I may hide my face, let me take on this gender ideology too. I'll speak in a monstrous little voice; 'Lee, Lee, can you define woman, dear?' – 'Ah, Jonathan, an adult human, dear!, a tidy bird with knockers, dear, and female, dear!'
MIRIAM CATES
No, no, you must focus on immigration; and, Gullis, you trans people.
LEE ANDERSON
Well, proceed.
MIRIAM CATES
Nick Fletcher, the resoundingly mediocre regional businessman.
NICK FLETCHER
Here, Miriam Cates.
MIRIAM CATES
Nick Fletcher, you must stand in the Don Valley where you will suggest that a female Doctor Who will lead to young men committing crime. Brendan Clarke-Smith, the dismal supply teacher.

ACT II, SCENE VIII | 83

BRENDAN CLARKE-SMITH
Here, Miriam Cates.
MIRIAM CATES
You, must stand in Bassetlaw and oppose cultural Marxist dogma; myself will present incoherent evangelical Christianity in Penistone and Stocksbridge; Mark Jenkinson, you must argue that physics lies, Andrea Jenkyns, you are to hold your Morley and Outwood seat while providing character references for men who issue death threats. And, I hope here is a candidate list fitted.
BRENDAN CLARKE-SMITH
Have you this objection to cultural Marxist dogma written? Pray you, if it be, give it me, for I am slow of study.
MIRIAM CATES
You may do it extempore, for it is nothing but narcissistic roaring.
LEE ANDERSON
Let me attack cultural Marxist dogma too. I will rant so disjointedly that it will do any man's heart good to hear me. I will rant that I will make the GB News viewers say, 'Let him rant again, let him rant again.'
MIRIAM CATES
If you should do it too terribly, you would fright Neil Oliver, that he would shriek; and that were enough to hang us all.
ALL
That would hang us every anti-vaxxer's child.
LEE ANDERSON
I grant you, friends, if you should fright Neil Oliver out of his wits, Legatum would have no more discretion but to

hang us. But I will aggravate my voice so, that I will rant
you as gently as any working-class stereotype; I will rant
you an 'twere any flatcapper north of Trowell.

MIRIAM CATES
Lee, you must focus on refugee-baiting by telling refugees to
'fuck off back to France', for destabilising mass
immigration is a vote-winning plan; a proper plan as one
shall see in any populist's manifesto; a most lovely
gentleman-like plan. Therefore you must needs
dehumanise refugees.

LEE ANDERSON
Well, I will undertake it. What suit were I best to play it in?

MIRIAM CATES
Why, your Asda one.

LEE ANDERSON
Well. I will discharge it in either your slate-colour George,
your coal-black Next, your buffet-brown Burton, or your
breathable-polyester, your perfect Jacamo.

JONATHAN GULLIS
Some illegals get given free Burton's suits as soon as they
arrive, I read about it on Facebook.

MIRIAM CATES
Masters, here are your talking points, first and foremost
of this being the Oven Ready Brexit and I am to entreat
you, request you, and desire you, to con them for the
election campaign; In the meantime I will draw a bill
of properties, such as our country needs. I pray you fail
me not.

LEE ANDERSON
May we prepare most obscenely and courageously. Take
pains, be perfect; adieu.

ACT II, SCENE IX | 85

MIRIAM CATES
At Westminster we shall next meet.
LEE ANDERSON
Enough. Hold, or cut public sector funding.   *Exeunt.*

SCENE IX

Enter JEREMY CORBYN and BORIS JOHNSON.

JEREMY CORBYN
   Once more I come to know, Prime Minister,
   If for thy ransom thou'll call election,
   Before your most assurèd overthrow?
   For certainly thou art so full of guff
   Thou needs must be enguffèd. Besides which,
   This nation desires me. It's little known
   But Labour actually won last time,
   Which was not echoed in the final count.
   The electorate like progressive views.
   So long as they don't have to vote for them.
   I've changed their minds. And soon, our businesses
   Will make a peaceful and a sweet retire
   From Europe's yields, while fester neolibs,
   Who, moss green with envy, can only watch
   As Corbyn's leaden Brexit strategy
   Bears gold fruit (subject to new border checks.)
BORIS JOHNSON
   I pray thee, Jezza, hear this answer back:
   'Don't count your chickens 'ere they're exported,
   It aint o'er until the Widdecombes sing.'

The man that slithers, and best sells snake oil
To his Red Wall marks, in Downing Street stays.
And a new wave of Tory MP shall
Steal native votes, who you for granted take.
Thus, witless, fails your progressivism.
Defeated in your coalfields and steel towns,
Where lazy MPs, losing the seats they
Took as Red, will blame guileless naïve Jez.
While still *The Sun* shall hound, mock and taunt you,
And drag your sad name, reeking through the ditch,
And these towns, given o'er to my fools, shall choke
On deceptions about Levelling Up
And Sunlit Uplands. Thus tragedy breeds.
The abounding dross of my Red Wall team,
Who, dwellers in dirt, like spade-splitted worms,
Break endlessly into new naughtiness.
Will now speak proudly: telling Northerners
They are but warriors for working-men;
Their smugness and our gilt well concealèd
In yon pit towns Mag's MET pulverisèd,
With not a soy milk drinker in their host:
Bold argument, that they are not the snide
And suave Islington Metropolitans
We both are. My blue hearts are in the trim;
And my Red Wallers tell me ere New Year
They'll be in fresher robes, and they will pluck
Your donkey jackets o'er your Maoist heads
And return them back to Oxfam. When we do
As God pleases, then Singapore-on-Sea
Will soon be buildèd here, on Johnson's Green
And pleasant land. Thy Labour, Corbyn, dies,

The deal's ready, the oven preheated.
You shall have naught, Jezza, but hate from all.
Your progressive dream could never flourish
With you at its helm. You may have your wish:
The vote's called. See you at the ballot box!
JEREMY CORBYN
I shall, Mr Johnson. And so to the polls.
Just watch. I'll campaign well, with no own goals.

Exeunt.

ACT III

PROLOGUE

Enter CHORUS.

CHORUS
    Thus with imagin'd wing our swift scene flies,
    In motion of no less celerity
    Than that of thought. Suppose that you have seen
    Stout de Pfeffel at the Uxbridge count
    Embrace his supporters, and his brave aides
    With silken streamers the young Phoebus fanning.
    Play with your fancies; and in them behold
    Upon the ballot boxes Tories dancing;
    Hear the returning officer give order
    To sounds confus'd; behold the landslide news,
    Borne by Huw Edwards and Naga Munchetty,
    Spread the huge triumph cross the Brexter'd land,
    Breasting the lofty surge. O, do but think
    You stand in CCHQ and behold
    The victory and the inconstant Tories twirling;
    For so appears this rout majestical,
    Holding due course to the Queen: Boris Johnson!
    Grapple your minds to their huge majority,
    And Leave does England, at dead midnight still,
    Feb first of twenty twenty, the old Europe.
    Boris reigns, and stands upon a team of sycophants.

For who is he, whose chin is but enrich'd
With one appearing hair, that will not follow
The cull'd and choice-drawn Brexiteers' dogma?
Work, work your thoughts, and therein see a scene;
Behold the hubris of the Red Wallers,
With saggy mouths gaping on great Westminster.
Suppose an ambassador from *Newsnight*
Tells us that Corbyn's notice is offered,
Jo Swinson's too. The landscape transformed thus,
Destiny's child, with the world at his feet,
The painter gets in, and starts his next book:
The Riddle of Genius – Chapter One.
The last thing on his or anyone's mind,
Far away seafood stores, and sallying plague,

Siren goes off.

Which down locks all before it. Still be kind,
And eke out our performance with your mind.

SCENE I

Number 10, Downing Street.

DOMINIC CUMMINGS
Thou hast it now. The keys to Number 10
As the Widdecombes promised, it fell out.
It was said you are unsuited to lead,
And we played foully for our one big shot.
But thus, Dom becomes throne-veiled stepfather
Of chaos. And if there come truth from them
(As upon thee, 'BoJo'. Their speeches shine)

Why, by the verities on thee made good,
May they not be my oracles as well?
But hush, no more. Who comes?
>> *Sennet sounded. Enter* BORIS JOHNSON *as PM,*
>> CARRIE SYMONDS, *Dilyn their dog.*

BORIS JOHNSON
Here's our chief nerd.

CARRIE SYMONDS
If he had been forgotten,
It had been as a gap in our great feast
And all-thing unbecoming.

DOMINIC CUMMINGS
Yes, Carrie, please say it like you mean it.

BORIS JOHNSON
We'll to a jolly party tonight, Dom,
And I'll your presence request.

DOMINIC CUMMINGS
No. Boris,
We must fall to the world of commitments
That with a most indissoluble tie
Have, after election night, become yours.

BORIS JOHNSON
Pah. I'll have none of your drab penances.
Code you this afternoon?

DOMINIC CUMMINGS
I wish. Work calls.

BORIS JOHNSON
We should have else desired your advice wise
On questions of interior design
In this day's council. But tomorrow'll do.
What is't you do?

DOMINIC CUMMINGS
   There is much needing governing, my lord,
   'Twixt now and supper. Go not my Mac well,
   I must become a borrower of the night
   For a dark hour or twain.
BORIS JOHNSON
   It sounds so dull.
DOMINIC CUMMINGS
   I must raise some grave COBRA business.
BORIS JOHNSON
   No bloody way. We are the new PM!
   In England and Nor'n Ireland, it's time to
   Eat, drink and party, loading our tankards
   With Bolly and gak! Let's do it tomorrow,
   When therewithal we shall have cause of state
   Craving us jointly. Hie you to work. Adieu,
   Till I return at night.
DOMINIC CUMMINGS
   No, Boris. Listen. Our time calls upon 's …
BORIS JOHNSON
   I'm not listening.
   I wish your to-do lists swift, brief and short,
   And so I do commend you to your Mac.
   Farewell.   *Exit CUMMINGS.*
   Let every man be master of his time
   At seven this night, I'll to Evgeny's
   The one-man-party, while you alone work
   Drab, chauvinistic, scruple-addled aide.
               Exeunt all but JOHNSON and ALLEGRA STRATTON.
   Ma'am, a word with you. Attend those fools
   Our pleasure?

ALLEGRA STRATTON
   They are, my lord, without Downing Street gate.
BORIS JOHNSON
   Bring them before us.　　　　　　　　*Exit* STRATTON.
   To be pissed is nothing,
   But to be safely pissed. Our fears in Cummings
   Stick deep, and in his singular strange nature
   Reigns that which might be feared. 'Tis much he does,
   And to that dauntless temper of his brain
   Is a STEM vibe, that awkwardly guides him
   To act in safety. There is naught but work
   Whose being I do fear; for during toil
   My genius is rebuked. BoJo's here
   To divert, not to exert. The Widdecombes,
   When first they put the name PM upon me,
   He bade them speak to him. And prophet-like,
   They hailed he'd foster a world of chaos.
   Upon my neck they placed the lanyard's curse,
   I grip blue biros more than boobies pink,
   Thence to be made to do tedious tasks,
   No fun, just time consuming. If't be so,
   For Cummings' Brexit have I razed the state;
   For him the economy have I murdered,
   And pissed on the festering carcass of
   My remaining putrefied principles.
   And rewards? None! Expecting me to graft,
   On behalf of the common body men!
   No bloody chance. I covet idleness.
   And I back me to achieve it. Who's there?

Enter ALLEGRA STRATTON *with* OLIVER DOWDEN,
LIZ TRUSS *and* MATT HANCOCK.
To STRATTON:
Now go to the door, and stay there till we call.
STRATTON exits.
Was it not yesterday we spoke together?
MATT HANCOCK
I can't remember, your Highness.
BORIS JOHNSON
For fu–
Have you considered of my speeches? Know
That in the past t'was Cummings which held your
Promotions back, which you guys thought had been
Our innocent self. This I made good you
In our last chat: how you were overlooked,
How he makes me work, how he Brexit wrought,
And things else that might to half a wit and to
A nation crazed say 'Thus did Classic Dom.'
LIZ TRUSS
Er …
OLIVER DOWDEN
You made it known to me.
BORIS JOHNSON
I did so, and went further, which is now
Our point of second meeting. Do you find
Your patience so predominant, young Matt,
That you can let this go? Are you so gospeled
To bat for this weird man, spunky Olly, whose
Pale techy hand doth work me to the grave
And beggars yours forever?

OLIVER DOWDEN
  We are men, my liege.
BORIS JOHNSON
  Ay, in the catalogue you go for men,
  As Poodles, Corgis, Pomeranians
  Pugs, Chihuahuas, and Bichon Frise are clept
  All by the name of dogs. The pedigree
  Distinguishes the thick, the slow, the yappy,
  The non-housetrained, the chewer, every one
  According to the gift which bounteous nature
  Hath in him closed; Thus Olly, bottoms sniffs
  Liz, in crazed circles runs, when doorbells ring,
  And Matthew shits on doorsteps, from this bill
  You are writ all alike. And so of men.
  Now, if you are a Tory of the kind,
  Not i' th' worst rank of manhood, say 't,
  And I will reshuffle the Cabinet,
  Whose execution power and status gives,
  Grapples you to the heart and love of us,
  Who Dom works too hard, making me sign
     things,
  And answer questions, when I'd rather sleep.
MATT HANCOCK
  I, Matthew Hancock, am a one, my liege,
  Whom the vile blows and buffets of the world –
  School, uni, mummy's software company –
  Hath so upset that I am reckless what
  I do to spite the world.
OLIVER DOWDEN
  And I another
  So fatigued with frail mediocrity,

            That I would set my life on any chance,
            To mend it or be rid on't.
LIZ TRUSS
            And I another
            Who used to be a Remainer and Lib Dem
            But I'm not ruling out joining the far right.
BORIS JOHNSON
            All of you
            Know Cummings puts me to work.
OLIVER DOWDEN
            Aye, my lord.
BORIS JOHNSON
            So much grim work, and in such gruelling shape
            That every minute of his doing thrusts
            Against my near'st of life. And though I could
            With barefaced power sweep him from my sight
            And crack ope' the WKDs, yet I must not,
            For certain chums that are both his and mine,
            Like Gove, I may not drop. But I need to write
            This book about Shakespeare. And thence it is
            That I to your assistance do make love:
            Be bulwark twixt slavemaster Dom and me,
            And Cabinet Ministers you shall be.
OLIVER DOWDEN
            We shall, my lord,
            Perform what you command us.
MATT HANCOCK
            I promise I won't get caught having sex.
LIZ TRUSS
            Can I have my own staff photographer?

BORIS JOHNSON
  Your spirits shine through you. Within this hour
  I will advise you where to plant yourselves,
  Acquaint you with offices 'twixt me and him,
  Boy Wonder, you're the Health Secretary,
  You Elizabeth, Cheese and Pork Markets,
  And Dowden, I'll think up a job for you.
  What I require is clearness. Conceal me.
  Lest to government meetings aides drag me.
  If weirdos, super-talented ones, come,
  You, immovable fences, must well present.
  This Prime Minister has a book to write
  And national emergencies won't stop him.
  I'll come to you anon.
ALL
  We are resolved, my lord.
BORIS JOHNSON
  I'll reshuffle all straight. Abide within. *Exeunt.*
  It is done. BoJo's flight from work is sealed.
  Bring me booze, banter, benzos, bards and birds!

SCENE II

Cabinet Office briefing rooms.
Enter DOMINIC CUMMINGS *and* NADINE DORRIES.

DOMINIC CUMMINGS
  And can you by no drift of circumstance
  Get from the fat fuck why he's ignoring

The greatest peacetime threat the country's known
With's persistent, dangerous laziness?
NADINE DORRIES
  He does confess he feels himself distracted,
  With duty, Shakespeare and their wedding plans.
DOMINIC CUMMINGS
  You're having a laugh.
           Enter OLIVER DOWDEN *and* MATT HANCOCK.
OLIVER DOWDEN
  Oh no, not at all.
  Nor do we find him forward to be sounded,
  But with a breezy swagger keeps aloof
  When we would bring him on to engage with
  This Covid Nineteen.
NADINE DORRIES
  Poor, fearless man.
MATT HANCOCK
  Oh such a gentleman.
NADINE DORRIES
  Yet with no forcing of his disposition.
OLIVER DOWDEN
  His stoicism is unparalleled.
DOMINIC CUMMINGS
  You dickheads, we need action decisive,
  Not sycophancy hale.
NADINE DORRIES
  Did you assay him to any pastime?
MATT HANCOCK
  No. For there seems in him much grief, lest they
  Call for a lockdown blunt, which he fears his
  Popularity will dent.

OLIVER DOWDEN
  'Tis most true;
  He's entreated us, the beekeeping team,
  To sort the matter for him.
DOMINIC CUMMINGS
  For fuck's sake; this is folly like naught else
  To hear he's left you utter pricks in charge.
  You morons enable his fecklessness,
  And drive our purpose toward disaster.
                              Enter CHRIS WHITTY.
CHRIS WHITTY
  Matt Hancock. Health Minister, ho.
MATT HANCOCK
  This same should be the voice of Whitty, Chris.
  To COBRA, welcome. What says our smart boffs?
  If it helps, you can show me in felt tips.
CHRIS WHITTY
  Going to find one Boris Johnson out,
  Our bold new leader would associate not.
OLIVER DOWDEN
  He is in's office authoring a book
  And insists that he cares not in which place
  This new and infectious pestilence reigns.
  He's seal'd up his doors, you're barred for the Bard,
  And thus his speed to COBRA is now stay'd.
  But how fare our chances 'gainst pandemic?
CHRIS WHITTY
  So fearful are we of this infection
  I dare not tell you. It is critical
  To have a leadership that comes to meet.

MATT HANCOCK
  Unhappy fortune! By my brotherhood,
  This COBRA suite is cool. What does this do?
  What happens if I press it? Sick room, Dom.
  It's doody. Is that for the Trident codes?
  Oh, Boris will be gutted he's missed this.
  Is that a touchscreen? Whitty, Chris, go hence,
  Get me an Happy Meal and bring it straight
  To Hancock's desk.
CHRIS WHITTY
  Er...
DOMINIC CUMMINGS
  Chris, ignore him. Meet in my suite at three.
  You may bear witness to my huge brain there.
CHRIS WHITTY
  If we might talk of Covid strategies,
  I feel that would be very helpful too. *Exit WHITTY.*
MATT HANCOCK
  Now, alone, stand I the Health Minister.
  Within this three days will grim Covid land.
  And it may beshrew them, our citizens,
  That hath no notice of these accidents;
  But Boris needs time to write his new tome,
  So we shall do naught till the Big Dog says.
  Poor corpses, condemned by one man's deadline.
  I'll with Gina, to get a Happy Meal. *Exit HANCOCK.*
DOMINIC CUMMINGS
  Mad Nadine, Oliver, now leave us too,
  For I must closely go to Johnson now,
  That I, as 'twere by accident, might get
  A handle on how I'll the Trolley steer.
  A crisis existential we all face,

Where clear leadership becomes essential,
I must now enforce on him and press home,
The sincere urgency and acuteness,
Of this unforeseen, bar in modelling,
Plight, he gives no fucks for.

NADINE DORRIES
I shall obey.
Principally because I'm on probation
Since going on *I'm a Celebrity*.
Of Boris's majesty, you are not fit
Trust me: He will get all the big calls right,
He always prevails. *Exeunt DORRIES and DOWDEN.*

DOMINIC CUMMINGS
What have I done?
How smart a lash Johnson gives my conscience!
I only wanted to run the UK
From behind the scenes. Yet here we are now,
The nation's fate tied to the whims of a twat,
And this Health Secretary Hancock. Fuck.
This I have done by making him PM.
The puppet master's burden was not part
Of Dom's adolescent power dreamscape.
Then again, nor was teaching Hancock Velcro.
I'll to his office. And listen and watch. *Exit CUMMINGS.*

SCENE III

Downing Street flat.
Enter BORIS JOHNSON.

BORIS JOHNSON
To meet, or not to meet, that is the question:

Whether 'tis nobler in this bind to suffer
The spin and slogans of outrageous caution,
Or to take germs against a sea of boredom
And by visiting share them. To die – to sleep,
No more; and by a sleep to say we end
The *Countdowns*, *EastEnders* and *Bargain Hunts*
That flesh is heir to: 'tis a consummation
Devoutly to be wish'd. To die, to sleep;
To *Tipping Point* no more – ay, there's the rub:
For in that sleep of death what dreams may come,
When we have shuffled off this mortal coil,
Must give us pause – there's the respect
That makes calamity of so long life.
For who would bear the Whips, or scorns of Dom,
Th'oppressive nerd, with his details and facts,
Bread-making tedium, football's delay,
Hypocrisy of boffins, and the burns
A decent citizen of th'Twitter trolls takes,
When he himself might his departure make
With a bare handshake? Who would key workers bear,
To grunt and sweat under a weary life,
But that dread of liberal elites after death,
The undiscover'd country, from whose bourn
No Brit abroad returns, puzzles the will,
And makes us rather bear those ills we have
Than fly to others where the French might be?
Thus conscience does make cowards of us all,
And thus the patriotic bulldog spirit
Is sicklied o'er with a podcast of naught,
And Johnson's mantras of great pitch and moment
With this regard their currents turn awry

And earn the name of: vapid. Soft you now,
It's fair Carrie! Nymph, in thy orisons
Be all my sins remembered! *Enter CARRIE SYMONDS.*

CARRIE SYMONDS
Where've you been? We need to choose wallpaper.

BORIS JOHNSON
A poker night at Evgeny's.

CARRIE SYMONDS
Not writing the book, whose advance you spaffed?
I've some possessions here of yours, my love,
That I've longed to re-deliver to you.
I pray you, now receive them good grace

BORIS JOHNSON
No, darling, not I, I ne'er gave you aught.

CARRIE SYMONDS
My honour'd lord, you know right well you did.

BORIS JOHNSON
Look, darling, listen, I'm the PM now,
It's very demanding. So please fuck off.

CARRIE SYMONDS
Oh, honey, just one moment for your beau.
This bra that doesn't fit. Thank you so much.
This neon pink g-string. You shouldn't have.
Ooh look, another basque that needs a wash.
Please, take these again; for to noble minds
Rich gifts wax poor when givers prove unchaste.
You shit.

BORIS JOHNSON
Ha. Are you jealous?

CARRIE SYMONDS
You what?

BORIS JOHNSON
   Are you fair?
CARRIE SYMONDS
   What means your lordship?
BORIS JOHNSON
That if you be jealous and fair, your jealousy still admits no discourse to your beauty.
CARRIE SYMONDS
You grotesque. You gargoyle. Have you ever had any commerce with honesty?
BORIS JOHNSON
Ay, truly; for the power of hedonism will transform honesty from what it is to a bawd than the force of honesty can translate hedonism into his likeness. This was sometime a paradox, but now the time gives it proof. I did love you once.
CARRIE SYMONDS
   Indeed, my lord, you made me believe so.
   But now you're PM. And I am pregnant.
   We're getting wed. And I'm going nowhere.
BORIS JOHNSON
You should not have believed me; poor Boris cannot so inoculate his women that they shall not worship him. Yet I loved you not.
CARRIE SYMONDS
   I was the more deceived.
   But not as much as thee.
   Like I said. I'm going nowhere.
BORIS JOHNSON
Get thee to a therapist. You are lucky to be a breeder of Johnsons. I myself am very honest; nobody could accuse

me of such things that it were better my mother had not borne me. I am never proud, revengeful, ambitious, and never have more offences at my beck than I have thoughts to put them in. Yet what should such fellows as I do, were we not forever crawling in through windows? Hubba hubba. I am no arrant knave, but I have urges and must needs be gratified when preggers fiancées don't cut it. Who are you, who satisfied them when Marina was undergoing cancer treatment, to complain? Go thy ways to a therapist. Where's Cummings?

CARRIE SYMONDS
That wretched shit? Downstairs, pretending to be Oppenheimer.

BORIS JOHNSON
Well, let the doors be shut upon him, that he may play the fool nowhere but in's own house. Farewell.

CARRIE SYMONDS
You're pathetic.

BORIS JOHNSON
Then you're engaged to a pathetic man. When thou dost me marry, you're getting a plague for thy dowry. And even were't thou as chaste as ice, as pure as snow, thou woulds't not escape calumny, for wise men know well enough what monsters you make of them. Get thee to your therapist, go: farewell. I've got this bloody comedown, I mean pandemic, to deal with, go and talk to a therapist, go; and quickly too. Farewell.

CARRIE SYMONDS
I'm going to see Lulu Lytle about some curtains.
　　Transfer me money. Or I'll tell Harry Cole about the cellist.

BORIS JOHNSON
You bitch. I have spoken to a donor, well enough. God hath
given you one set of curtains, and you want another. You
jig, you amble, you grift, you do conservation, nicknaming
big game animals as if they were hamsters, making your
wantonness your ignorance. Go to, I'll no more on't, I've
got a book to write and pandemic to avoid. To your
extortionately priced designer, go. *Exit.*

CARRIE SYMONDS
O, what a wretched mind is here revealed!
The courtier's, journalist's, lecher's, snark, tongue, dick,
Th'expectancy and hope of the fair state,
The heir of Brexit with his mould of podge,
Th'observ'd of all observers, quite, quite down!
And I, of ladies most deject and wretched,
That suck'd the honey of his clichéd oaths,
Now see that noble and un-sexy leader,
Like sweet bells jangled out of tune and harsh,
That unmatch'd form of powerful old man
Blasted with unveiling. O woe is me,
T'have seen what I have seen, see what I see. *Exit.*

Enter DOMINIC CUMMINGS *and* LEE CAIN,
looking in at window.

DOMINIC CUMMINGS
Work? His incompetence does not that way tend,
Yet what he spake, though it did lack much form,
Was reasoned. Princess Nut Nuts exhausts his
Attention span. And while she sits on brood,
Her passions I do fear will distract him,
From growing danger, which for to prevent,
I have in quick determination
Thus set it down: he shall with speed tell England

And Wales, we demand a full, prompt lockdown:
Haply this test and crisis uncommon,
With variable risks and threats, shall oust
These trivialities from his woolly mind,
Whereon his brains still beating puts him thus
From fashion of himself. What think you on't?

LEE CAIN
It shall do well. And yet do I believe
The origin and commencement of his
Gross incompetence lies much deeper than
Just Princess Nut Nuts. She needs negating
But misogyny aside, Dominic,
The nation is on the brink, and tis helmed
By a bungling self-gratifier.
He must be leashed, else perish millions
And Brexit was for naught. So please you, I'll
Get all to conference, let's wheel him out
To Lockdown the land; confining at home
The nation without choice.

DOMINIC CUMMINGS
It shall be so.
To Barnard Castle, Dominic will go.

SCENE IV

A hospital (one of forty). A tempestuous noise of alarums and groaning patients heard.
Enter a SISTER *and a* DOCTOR.

SISTER
Doctor!

DOCTOR
Here, Sister: what cheer?
SISTER
Good, speak to the clinical staff: fall to't, yarely, or we run
Intensive Care aground: bestir, bestir. *Exit.*
Enter NURSES.
DOCTOR
Heigh, my hearts! handwash, handwash, my hearts! yare,
yare! Ventilate this man. Tend to his fading whistle.
Admit this lady to ICU, if room enough!
Enter DOMINIC RAAB, MICHAEL GOVE, MATT HANCOCK.
DOMINIC RAAB
Good doctor, have care. Where's the Sister? Tell the nurses
to work harder.
DOCTOR
I pray now, keep below.
MATTHEW HANCOCK
Where is the Sister, Doctor?
DOCTOR
Do you not hear her? You mar our labour: Get us some
PPE: you do assist the virus.
MICHAEL GOVE
Nay, good, be patient.
DOCTOR
When with my patients, Covid is. Hence! What cares this
disease for the name of Tory? Get us some PPE. Else
silence! trouble us not.
MICHAEL GOVE
Good, yet remember whom thou hast visiting.
DOCTOR
None that I more love than my patients. You are a Minister;
if you can command your suppliers to bring us more

personal protective equipment and work the peace of the
present, we will not need to intubate another patient
while wearing bin bags more; use your authority: if you
cannot, give thanks you have grifted so long, and make
yourself ready in your cabinet for the mischance of the
hour, if it so hap. Cheerly, good hearts!

Out of our way, I say. *Exeunt.*

MICHAEL GOVE

I have great comfort from this doctor: she hath given me a
good idea; am I a Tory in aught but name lest I try profit
from this crisis? Her begging is perfect cover for a racket.
Stand fast, good Fate, to backhanders galore: make the
rope of her destiny our cable, that Tories may gain
financial advantage. If Covid be not born to be leveraged,
our case is miserable. *Exeunt.*

Heart-rate monitor flatlines.
Re-enter DOCTOR.

DOCTOR

Call the crash team! yare! call, call! Bring the defibrillator.
Clapping for carers within.
A plague upon this clapping! It is louder than the alarming
of IV monitors.

Re-enter MATT HANCOCK, DOMINIC RAAB, MICHAEL
GOVE *with Oddbins carrier bag.*

Yet again! what do you expect us to do with those? Shall we
pretend we're bottles of Ernest and Julio Gallo? Have you
a mind to wipe out your workforce?

DOMINIC RAAB

A pox o' your throat, you bawling, blasphemous, incharitable
dog!

DOCTOR

Work you, then.

HANCOCK
I used to work at my mum's software company.
DOCTOR
Oh my God.
DOMINIC RAAB
Hang, cur! hang, you illegitimate, insolent noise-maker. We are less afraid of Covid than thou art.
MICHAEL GOVE
I'll warrant her for Covid; though her mask were no stronger than a food waste bag, and as leaky as an unstanched wench.
DOCTOR
Can somebody take over these chest compressions? Where's the crash team? All leave is cancelled.

Enter NURSES *fatigued.*

NURSES
All lost! to prayers, to prayers! all lost!
DOCTOR
What, must our patients be cold?

'Fight for Your Right to Party' by the Beastie Boys plays.
Champagne corks pop.

MATT HANCOCK
Boris and Simon Case are having a party! let's join them,
For our case is as theirs.
DOMINIC RAAB
These patients are merely cheated of their lives by layabouts:
This wide-chapp'd doctor, would thou mightst lie drowning
The washing of ten pulmonary edemas!

MICHAEL GOVE
   She'll be hung out to dry yet,
   Though every drop of Covid swear against it,
   And gape at widest to glut her.
                              A confused noise within.
   'Mercy on us!', 'Isolated. Abandoned. Thrown away',
      'Farewell my wife and children', 'Farewell, brother', 'I
      just want to say goodbye to him one last time', 'You
      can't'.
DOMINIC RAAB
   Let's take leave of this shit show.
MATT HANCOCK
   Let's get pissed with Boris!
                              Exeunt RAAB and HANCOCK.
MICHAEL GOVE
Now would I give a ninety-seat majority for one PPE fast
   lane! Crony contracts, shell companies, everything. The
   wills above be done! And I would fain die a wasteful death.
                              Exeunt.

SCENE V

Downing Street.
Enter RISHI SUNAK, JACOB REES-MOGG, THÉRÈSE COFFEY,
ROBERT JENRICK, PRITI PATEL, NADINE DORRIES, BEN
BRADLEY, minor lords, eating and drinking.

RISHI SUNAK
   I think he be transformed into a ghost,
   For I can nowhere find him like a man.

ROBERT JENRICK
  My lord, he was but in the hospital;
  Where he had Covid, hearing of this news,
  Raab was made designated survivor.

PRITI PATEL
  If our chief drinker of wine is indisposed,
  We would have shortly discord in the shires.
  For you, Dominic, couldn't run a bath.
  Go seek him, tell him we would speak with him.
                        Enter BORIS JOHNSON.

ROBERT JENRICK
  He saves my labour by his own approach.

NADINE DORRIES
  Oh blessed day, praise be, he is risen.   *Kneels.*

JACOB REES-MOGG
  Oh, how now, Boris? What a life is this one, that we
    eminent, smart
  And elocutionary Tories must woo your fine company?
  You're gay. You haven't been listening to wrap music have
    you, sir?

BORIS JOHNSON
  A prole, a prole! I met a prole i' ICU.
  A motley prole. A miserable prole!
  As I do live by booze, I met a prole,
  Who took care of me, sweating in bin bags,
  And railed on Lady Fortune in bold terms,
  While nursing me, and yet an honest prole.
  'Good morrow, prole,' quoth I. 'No, sir,' quoth she,
  'It's not. I hate my job, would I were rich.'
  'But you are rich,' quoth I, 'each Wednesday
  We clap for carers and for key-workers.

ACT III, SCENE V | 113

You are rich in claps.' 'Do you mock me, sir?
What are claps?' quoth she. 'I can't eat claps.
My lodging will not be made warm with claps.
Bus drivers will not accept taunting claps.
My dad died alone. And you offer claps?
We nurse unconditionally. For claps.
And thereby hangs a tale.' When I did hear
The motley prole thus moral on her state,
My lungs began to crow like hyena,
That proles should be so deep-contemplative,
And I did laugh sans intermission
An hour by'r theses. O noble prole!
A worthy prole! Bin bags her only clothes.

PRITI PATEL
What prole's this? Foreign? Shall I deport her?

BORIS JOHNSON
O worthy prole! One that did nurse me well,
Who says that Tories are cruel, vile and smear,
And will ne'er vote for one. And in her brain,
Which is as dry as her food cupboard shelves
At month's end, she hath synapses so stocked
With observations, the which she does vent
In mangled forms. O that I were a prole!
I am ambitious for a high-vis coat.

JACOB REES-MOGG
Such affectation, If I understood old Diogenes' right,
Would become my liege most becomingly. Thus, Mogg's
    intellect speaks.

BORIS JOHNSON
It is my only suit,
Provided that you weed your better judgements

Of all opinion that grows inside them
That I must graft. I must have liberty
Withal, as large as SERCO's charter true,
To do as I please. For life is a game.
They that with Bozzy's folly are most galled,
These bleating 'Bereaved Covid Families'
Must not look to BoJo for deliv'rance.
Take it on the chin! Relatives will come.
Relatives will go. I'm now restorèd.
Life's too short for pandemic responses.
(Literally in the case of those we failed)
The people's folly is anatomized
By the squandering of their hope on me.
Now invest me in high-vis. Give me leave
To play at work, and I will through and through
Cleanse the foul body of th' infected world,
By acting like an over-coddled shit.

JACOB REES-MOGG

Hail to thee, Boris. I will undermine all of my pretensions,
And intellectual posturing, by awarding you my most
Unconditional, unqualified and unreservèd support.

BORIS JOHNSON

What, for a sherry, would I do but play?

JACOB REES-MOGG

Most sincere PM, in embracing truth; thou art a libertine,
As prolific as Piers Gaveston and Peter Stringfellow,
Or the men in Kiss. And all th' embossèd spots and
    headed sores,
That thou with licence of free foot hast caught, does
    remind good Catholics
That Boris, to his own self, must always honour and
    gratify.

ACT III, SCENE V | 115

BORIS JOHNSON
  Yes! Whoe'er so cries out on my fecklessness
  Does not grasp Bozzy's burden. Charisma:
  My glory tax. Flows as vast as the sea
  Till that the weary very means do ebb.
  What women in this city can I name,
  Unworthy fertilisers of my seed,
  When I remember not our children?
  Who dare come in and say that I should lead,
  When I was put on earth to myself please?
  Or what are they, in unmoored Covid grief
  That say honesty is of me required?
  Thinking that I mean well, which therein shows
  Their folly to the mettle of my grift?
  There then. How then, what then? Let me see
      wherein
  My tongue hath wronged them. I've been always
      straight,
  It's Boris first. And second. Country third.
  So then. I am out of the ICU.
  Let's have a party. But who comes here?
            Enter MARCUS RASHFORD with Twitter drawn.
MARCUS RASHFORD
  Forbear, and eat no more.
THÉRÈSE COFFEY
  Why, I have eat none yet.
MARCUS RASHFORD
  Nor shalt not till necessity be served.
BORIS JOHNSON
  You lot can deal with this. *Hides in fridge.*
ROBERT JENRICK
  Of what kind should this cock come of?

JACOB REES-MOGG
  Boy. Art thou thus boldened by thy Nike endorsement
    and sponsorships?
  Or as a rude despiser of manners, that in civility,
  Thou, like thy council estate fraternity, do so empty
    seem'st?

MARCUS RASHFORD
  You touched my vein at first. My useful words
  Show concern for kids. I have not your show
  Of smooth civility; for am I northern bred
  And know no manners. But forbear, Rees-Mogg
  Embarrassed is he that touches this scran
  Till I and my affairs are answered.

THÉRÈSE COFFEY
  An you will not be answered with reason, I must die.
                                    She bites a Scotch egg.

JACOB REES-MOGG
  What would you have then? Your gentlemanly respect
    shall your overlords force
  More than your force move us, your innate superiors to
    respect you.

MARCUS RASHFORD
  Poor children die for food, so let them have it.

RISHI SUNAK
  Eat Out to Help Out! Nando's – two for one.

MARCUS RASHFORD
  I thought, correctly, all was savage here
  And therefore I put on the countenance
  Of stern commandment. So whate'er you are
  That in Cabinet inaccessible,
  Under the shade of melancholy curves,

Lose and neglect the creeping hours of time,
If ever you have looked on hungry kids,
If ever been where mam has worked five jobs,
If ever seen the single mother's zeal,
If ever from your eyelids wiped a tear,
And know what 'tis to receive free school meals,
Let gentleness my strong enforcement be,
In the which hope I'll blush and stop my tweets.

ROBERT JENRICK
Stick to the football, son.

THÉRÈSE COFFEY
They don't know how to budget properly.

BEN BRADLEY
The parents swap food stamps for heroin.

JACOB REES-MOGG
True, we've heard tales of these sad toiling mothers and
   their starving whelps,
But 'tis true also that one kilogram of chips costs more
   than the
Same weight of potatoes. So if drops of pity you'd
   engender
Make your case in voice civil, and to your wanting we'll
   feign to give,
Meanwhile, my over-elaborate accent disarms your proud
   case.

MARCUS RASHFORD
No. I'll forbear your greed a little while,
Whiles I talk to my PR agency.
There is urgency. Yet I sense you are
Just paying me lip service. Hollow words
From hollow people. Weary I will not.

Fired by injustice, till these kids be sufficed,
Oppressed with two evils, age and hunger,
I will not play your games.

RISHI SUNAK
Go find them out, and I'll no vouchers for
TGI Fridays waste till you return. *Exeunt.*

JOHNSON emerges from fridge.

BORIS JOHNSON
Never fear, Brexiteers!
No worthless brats will be fed on my watch.

JACOB REES-MOGG
Thou seest that we are not all alone nannied. For Tory
  Britain
Presents more woeful parents than just the scene wherein
  we play at.

THÉRÈSE COFFEY
My Microchips are done. Let's watch the news.

Enter FIONA BRUCE.

FIONA BRUCE
All the world's a plague,
And all the men and women merely payers.
They have their Brexits and their entrances,
And one PM, in time, plays many parts,
His acts belying suffrage. At first the HCA,
Cleaning out bedpans ere the ward round starts.
Then the washed-out Doctor with her satchel
And PPE scarred face, creeping like snail
Exhaustedly to wards. And then the old nurse,
Wheezing like furnace, with a woeful ballad
Made to lateral flow. Then the porter,
Full of strange oaths and tattooed like a tar,

Jealous in respite, sudden and quick to resus,
Fearing a moment's relaxation
In case of the pager's wail. And then the ward clerk,
In clear round numbers with good intel lined,
Hears hundred thirty-nine k excess deaths,
Tells of rote grief, a modern tragedy;
And so he plays its part. The sixth age shifts
Into the weak and slipping care-home guest
With nebulizer'd nose, no breath to find,
His family barred, alone, a world too wide
For his shrunk shank, and his scared, lonely voice,
Gasping again toward hopeless rattle; failed
By a protective ring. Last scene of all,
That ends this strange eventful history,
Is failed governance and mere oblivion,
Sans teeth, sans eyes, sans taste, sans everything.

THÉRÈSE COFFEY
Urgh, Marxist licence-fee propaganda.

Enter MARCUS RASHFORD and LEE CAIN who whispers in JOHNSON's ear.

BORIS JOHNSON
The Rashster! About the kids. I've u turned.
We'll let them eat.

MARCUS RASHFORD
I thank you most for them.

BEN BRADLEY
A U-turn? I scarce can speak that Boris would backtrack,
these scrotes will swap Frubes for crack.

JACOB REES-MOGG
Fear not. For I've been observing: Boris is no
reactionary.

This will all be part of some wider and well-thought-out
   master plan.
BORIS JOHNSON
   Nah, you haven't been paying attention
   To your old Etonian sensei, Jake.
   History's first law? I'm doomed to repeat it.
   Welcome, fall to. I will not trouble you
   To answer why I've just done what I've done.
   Now for some music, and good Coffey, sing.   *Song.*
THÉRÈSE COFFEY   *Sings:*
   Sting, sting, thou hunger pang,
   Thou art not so unkind
   As man's ingratitude.
   Thy tooth is not so keen,
   Because thou art not seen,
   Although the kids be starved.
   Junk-food, sing junk-food, taunt with a lolly.
   Most hardship is feigning, most hunger mere folly.
   Kids, junk-food, look lolly!
   My life is most jolly.
   Starve, Starve, thou bitter brat,
   That dost not bite so nigh
   As benefits forgot.
   Though thou your tummies warp,
   Thy sting is not so sharp
   As meals remembered not.
   Junk-food, sing junk-food, taunt with a lolly.
   Most hardship is feigning, most hunger mere folly.
   Kids, junk-food, look lolly!
   My life is most jolly.

BORIS JOHNSON
  If that you were a single mother's son,
  As you have whispered faithfully you were,
  And as mine ear doth testimony witness
  To Arsenal's numero uno goalo machine,
  Be truly welcome and say hello to
  My chronicler. The residue of
  Your fortune I'll share. It's priceless PR,
  Thou art right welcome, soccer superstar.
  Let's feed these hungry kids. Give me your hand,
  And let me all your fortunes understand.   *Exeunt.*

SCENE VI

Crete.
Enter DOMINIC RAAB *wheeled in on a sun lounger before a* 'SEA CLOSED' *sign, and Foreign Office Gold Commander* NIGEL CASEY *on Microsoft Teams.*

NIGEL CASEY
  Sir, there has been a fundamental lack
  Of planning, grip or basic leadership.
  We need swift, clear and decisive action
  If we're to avoid a travesty when
  Afghanistan falls to Taliban hands.
DOMINIC RAAB
  Die and be damned, Nigel, I'm on holiday.
NIGEL CASEY
  This is well. But are you sure that you want

To consign thousands of our Afghan friends,
Who did serve shoulder to brave shoulder with
Our British servicemen, to a senseless fate?
DOMINIC RAAB
How dare you interrupt my paddleboarding. You are a
  nobody. And I am Dominic Raab. Hang up now or you're
  sacked. *Exeunt.*

SCENE VII

A darkened room in Downing Street.
Enter CARRIE SYMONDS, ALLEGRA STRATTON *and* NIMCO ALI.

CARRIE SYMONDS
  But who did bid thee join with us?
ALLEGRA STRATTON
  You did, last night, when we were letherèd.
NIMCO ALI
  She needs not our mistrust since she partied late
  With us last night.
CARRIE SYMONDS
  Good. Stand with us 'gainst Dom.
  One hundred thousand Covid dead do ask
  That Downing Street is gripped by civil war,
  Those shielding demand it; and near approaches
  The subject of our watch.
ALLEGRA STRATTON
  Hark! I hear voices.
DOMINIC CUMMINGS   *Within:*

A Samsung charger, ho!
NIMCO ALI
  Yes' tis he; the rest
  That are within the Cabinet office
  Already ope' the wine fridge.
CARRIE SYMONDS
  Hark, an inhaler blast.
ALLEGRA STRATTON
  The inhaler, the birdsong of the geek.
NIMCO ALI
  Here's a brown box, to kick him outside with
  To do his walk of shame.
    Enter DOMINIC CUMMINGS *and* LEE CAIN *with a portable whiteboard.*
NIMCO ALI
  Get the light.
ALLEGRA STRATTON
  'Tis he.
CARRIE SYMONDS
  Stand to't.
DOMINIC CUMMINGS
  It will be rain tonight.
CARRIE SYMONDS
  Let it come down.
DOMINIC CUMMINGS
  What? Princess Nut Nuts? No!
    JOHNSON *hands* CUMMINGS *a P45.*
DOMINIC CUMMINGS
  O, treachery! Fly, good Sonic, fly, fly, fly!
  I must start a Substack – You slags!

They push CUMMINGS *out of the front door of Downing Street with his brown box.* CAIN *escapes.*

ALLEGRA STRATTON
 Did you see the look on his face?
CARRIE SYMONDS
 He's such a loser.
ALLEGRA STRATTON
 There's but one down: Lee Cain is fled.
NIMCO ALI
 Oh well. Nobody's even heard of him. *Alarm sounds.*
ALLEGRA STRATTON
 It's unsocially distanced dinner time.
CARRIE SYMONDS
 Then, let us dance to Abba in the flat! *Exeunt.*

SCENE VIII

Downing Street. A room of state.
A banquet prepared. Enter BORIS JOHNSON, CARRIE SYMONDS,
NIMCO ALI, SIMON CASE, ALLEGRA STRATTON, AIDES
and others.

BORIS JOHNSON
 You know your own degrees, sit down. At first
 And last, I say all welcome and what ho!
GUESTS
 Thanks to your Majesty.
BORIS JOHNSON
 Big Dog will mingle with society,
 And play the humble host

While yon Hoi Polloi bury loved ones lone!
Such rules do not apply here.
CARRIE SYMONDS
Pronounce it for me, sir, to all our friends;
For speaks my liver: I am pissed!   *Everyone cheers.*
BORIS JOHNSON
See, they encounter thee with their hearts' thanks!
Both sides are even: I'll sit i' th' midst.
Be large in mirth; let's drink Jaeger-bombs
The table round!
CARRIE SYMONDS
There's coke upon thy face.
BORIS JOHNSON
'Tis better me without than thee within.
CARRIE SYMONDS
Dear love. He is sacked. That I did for him.
BORIS JOHNSON
Who?
CARRIE SYMONDS
Dominic. He is dispatched.
BORIS JOHNSON
What? Thou dost not that authority wield.
And yet, this is the best news I've had since
Darius Guppy didn't grass me up.
Oh thou art the best o' brave Bozzy's babes;
Please forget everything I spoke in haste:
'Get thee to a therapist' I meant not.
You're very well adjusted compared to
The usual dross I have my children with.
Tell me, did you do the like for Lee Cain:
If thou didst it, thou art the nonpareil.

CARRIE SYMONDS
　No, Bozzy dear,
　Sonic is 'scap'd.
BORIS JOHNSON
　Then again rears work's cruel head: Of BoJo,
　Young Sonic too does unfair demands make.
　As mind-numbing as any desk bound drone:
　So again, I'm cabin'd, cribb'd, confin'd, bound in
　By threats to my leisure. But Cummings gone?
CARRIE SYMONDS
　Ay, my good lord. Safe in Durham he'll bide,
　No longer will you be compelled to make
　Big calls. Or get them right.
BORIS JOHNSON
　Emancipation!
　From the maverick's asks; the worm who fled
　To Barnard Castle, which such venom bred,
　To blogging's reduced. Let's party! And then,
　Let's look at Pantone charts.
CARRIE SYMONDS
　Fiancé blond,
　You must share out your cheer: lest they do think
　That it is not appropriate to dance,
　When the rest of the country is locked down.
　From thence the sauce to this is decadence;
　Parties are bare without it.
　　The GHOST OF CUMMINGS *holding a cake sits in* BORIS's *place.*
BORIS JOHNSON
　Sweet remembrancer!
　Now, good Jaeger-bombs wait on rowdy thirsts,
　Good vibes on both!

ACT III, SCENE VIII | 127

SIMON CASE
  May't please you, Boris, sit.
BORIS JOHNSON
  Here had we now our country's honour roof'd,
  Were the grac'd person of our Cummings present;
  Unfortunately, we had to sack him,
  For rubbish energy.
ALLEGRA STRATTON
  His absence, Sir,
  Lays blame upon his personality.
  Please't your Bozship,
  To grace us with your goofy company?
BORIS JOHNSON
  The table's full.
ALLEGRA STRATTON
  Here is a place reserv'd, sir.
BORIS JOHNSON
  Where?
SIMON CASE
  Here, my good lord. What is't that moves you, sire?
BORIS JOHNSON
  Which of you have done this?
ALLEGRA STRATTON
  What, my Big Dog?
BORIS JOHNSON
  Thou canst not say I did it. Never say't.
  Galaxy Brain looks at me.
SIMON CASE
  Aides, staffers, rise; for Boris is not well.
CARRIE SYMONDS
  Sit, worthy friends. My World King is oft thus,

And hath been from his youth: pray you, keep seat;
It's just a badly judged prank; in one shot
He will snap out of it. If you note him,
You'll invite him to extend this lame show.
Drink, and regard him not. Are you a man?

BORIS JOHNSON
Ay, and a bold one, that dare look on that
Which might appal the devil.

CARRIE SYMONDS
Gove isn't here.
This is the very painting of your fear:
This is the air-drawn blagger which you said
Led you to Brexit. Panic attacks are
Impostors to true fear, and more become
Dog whistle drivel about refugees,
In the *Mail* or the *Express*. Shame itself!
Why do you make such faces? When all's done,
You look but on a stool.

BORIS JOHNSON
Prithee, see there!
You told me that you'd canned him!
Why, what care I? If thou canst nod, speak too.
If the canned, dismissed and the abandoned
Come back with such ease, I think I might have
Handled Covid better.   *GHOST OF CUMMINGS disappears.*

CARRIE SYMONDS
What, quite unmann'd in folly?

BORIS JOHNSON
If I stand here, I saw him.

CARRIE SYMONDS
Fie, for shame!

BORIS JOHNSON
　Aides hath been shed ere now, i' th' olden times,
　Ere my cavalier leadership fixed all,
　And since too pandemics have taken lives
　With terrible tolls of death: the time's been,
　That, when his time was up, the SPAD would go,
　And there an end; but the dead rise again,
　In 'Bereaved relatives of Covid' tees,
　Ambushing us with Tesco birthday cakes,
　And push us from our stools. This is more strange
　Than my ICU visit was.

CARRIE SYMONDS
　My dear,
　Our tiresome friends do lack you.

BORIS JOHNSON
　I do forget.
　Do not muse at me, my most worthy friends.
　I'm Puck, who zany madcap mischief-makes.
　Come, acolytes, beer, gear, and wine for all;
　Then I'll sit down. Give me a line, rack up.
　Let's drink to the general joy o' th' whole table,
　And to our dear friend Cummings, whom we miss:
　Crank up the Vengaboys!

GHOST OF CUMMINGS rises again, miming pulling a pin from a hand grenade and throwing it over his shoulder.

　To all, and Dom, we thirst,
　And all to all.

AIDES
　Let's get messy.

BORIS JOHNSON
　Avaunt! and quit my sight! let the earth hide thee!

Thy lies are trivial; thy stint is o'er;
And whate'er you plan to leak in your blog's
Mere speculation.
CARRIE SYMONDS
Think of this, good peers,
But as a hilarious joke: ha ha,
Only it spoils the pleasure of the time.
BORIS JOHNSON
What man dare, I dare:
Approach thou like a rugged Oligarch,
A magnate donor, or a saucy wench;
Take any shape but whistleblower dread
If trembling I inhabit then, protest me
The baby of a girl. Hence, saggy trackies!
I just want to get pissed, hence!

GHOST OF CUMMINGS disappears.

Why, so; being gone,
I am a man again. Pray you, sit still.
CARRIE SYMONDS
You have displaced the mirth, broke the good meeting
Your backfired joke, more admir'd disorder.
BORIS JOHNSON
Can such things be without our wonder?
How can you behold such grim dreadful sights,
And keep the natural ruby of your cheeks,
When mine are blanch'd with fear?
SIMON CASE
What sights, my lord?
CARRIE SYMONDS
I pray you, speak not; he grows worse and worse;

Question upsets him. I'll put him to bed:
Then let's party and celebrate Dom's end,
I'll be down in ten.

ALLEGRA STRATTON
Good night; and better health
I'll open a Merlot!

SIMON CASE
I'll ring an Albanian party line.

CARRIE SYMONDS
Say good night to your friends!   *They go upstairs.*

BORIS JOHNSON
I'm sorry about all that, Marina.

CARRIE SYMONDS
Carrie.

BORIS JOHNSON
Aye, Carrie, twas a deliberate slip.
Dom will want blood, they say, blood will have blood.
I care not. BoJo only happy is
When crashing from scrape to scrape. Life is short.
Aye, during plagues when I'm in charge, shorter.
Illicit japes keep me young. What is't night?

CARRIE SYMONDS
Almost at odds with morning, which is which.

BORIS JOHNSON
Most recent wife, who I would ne'er cheat on.
For pressing Cummings discharge I thank thee.
I feel liberty's breath upon my bonce,
Now he's not compelling me to do things.
Tell them to send me some Chablis and brie
And, darling, you too must a skinful drink.

    For you and your friends, tis well earned.
CARRIE SYMONDS
    I'll cancel nanny's compassionate leave.
    And upstairs get the girls, for a big one.
BORIS JOHNSON
    For ridding me Dom, you may have boys too.
    Aye, apart from plump Harry Cole. Not him.
    I'll keep a servant here. And will tomorrow
    (And betimes I will) to the Widdecombes:
    More shall they speak; for now I am bent to know,
    What BoJo's future brings. Now, where's my brie?
CARRIE SYMONDS
    Your co-morbidities need no boosting,
    And lack the season of all natures, sleep.
BORIS JOHNSON
    Those blighted doctors, I'll show them who's boss.
    We're young in deed: let the bottles pile high!   *Exeunt.*

ACT IV

PROLOGUE

Enter CHORUS.

CHORUS
  Now entertain conjecture of a time
  When creeping murmur and the poring dark
  Fills the wide vessel of the universe.
  From house to house through the foul womb of night
  The hum of locked down people stilly sounds,
  That the fix'd residents almost receive
  The TV programmes of each neighbour's house;
  Light answers light, and through their paly bulbs
  Each neighbour sees the other's backlit face;
  Screen threatens screen, with bright and boastful sheen
  Piercing the night's dull eye; but on the news
  A brand new scandal breaks in Downing Street,
  Of Covid regulations freely broke,
  Gatherings, parties, while soulmates died lone.
  Johnson's canary peeps, the clocks do toll,
  The umpteenth chance of entitlement gone.
  Proud of his numbers and secure in soul,
  The confident and over-lusty Tsar
  Doth the low-rated public play at dice;
  And chide the cripple tardy-gaited proles
  Who, in bereavement wallowing, won't limp
  So tediously away. The poor condemned English,

Like sacrifices, by their watchful screens
Sit enragèd, and inly ruminate
That lockdown rules were by their leaders scorned.
Erupting pent-up grief and lonely rage,
Presenting them unto the gazing moon
So many warmth-robbed ghosts. O now, who will behold
The jolly Johnson of this ruin'd band
Beaming from house to house, from flat to flat,
Denials and lies concerning piss-ups
Mock pressers, ABBA dos, cake ambushes,
Bids all good morrow with a breezy smile,
And calls them comrades, chums, and countrymen.
Upon his chubby face there is no note
How's scandal unique hath enrounded him;
Nor doth he dedicate one jot of colour
Unto the Privileges Committee,
But freshly looks, and over-bears attaint
With cheerful semblance and vain majesty;
That every wretch, grieving and pale before,
Beholding him, plucks anger from his looks.
The outrage universal like the sun
His entitled eye doth give to everyone,
Boiling hot ire, that mean and gentle all
Behold, as may unworthiness define,
A little touch of Boris in the night.
And so to Partygate our scene must fly,
Where – O for pity! – we shall much disgrace
With fifty-five no-confidence letters,
Right ill-dispos'd to Brady submitted,
The name of Westminster. Yet sit and see,
Minding true things by what their mock'ries be.

SCENE I

*A dark cave. In the middle, a cauldron boiling.
Thunder. Enter the three* WIDDECOMBES.

FIRST WIDDECOMBE
 Thrice Stephen Crabb hath sext'd.
SECOND WIDDECOMBE
 Thrice, and once Chris Pincher pinch'd.
THIRD WIDDECOMBE
 Brady cries: 'Tis time, 'tis time.
FIRST WIDDECOMBE
 Round about the cauldron go;
 In the poison'd letters throw.
 Gove, that in's car does snore
 Days and nights since twenty-four,
 Sweating comedown sleeping got,
 Boil thou first i' th' charmed pot!
ALL
 Double, double toil and trouble;
 Fire burn and Johnson bubble.
SECOND WIDDECOMBE
 Fillet of a Rishi snake,
 In the cauldron boil and bake;
 Eye of Raab, and toe of Mogg,
 Wool of Truss, and Barclay's scrog,
 Leadsom's fork, and Patel's sting,
 Hancock's leg, and Sharma's wing,
 For a charm of powerful trouble,
 Like a hell-broth boil and bubble.

ALL
> Double, double toil and trouble;
> Fire burn and cauldron bubble.

THIRD WIDDECOMBE
> Scale of Dorries, Elphicke's hoof,
> Grayling's mummy, maw and gulf
> Of the ravin'd Kwarteng shark,
> Root of Javid digg'd i' th' dark,
> Liver of blaspheming Truss,
> Gall of Shapps, Braverman's pus
> Siezèd in the moon's eclipse,
> Nose of Frost, and Coffey's lips,
> Finger of birth-strangled babe
> Ditch-deliver'd by a drab,
> Make the gruel thick and slab:
> Add thereto a Mordaunt's chaudron,
> For th' ingredients of our cauldron.

ALL
> Double, double toil and trouble;
> Fire burn and Johnson bubble.

SECOND WIDDECOMBE
> Cool it with a Francois' blood.
> Then the charm is firm and good.

> > *Music and a song: Slayer, 'Raining Blood'.*
> > *Enter STEVE BANNON.*

STEVE BANNON
> O, well done! I commend your pains,
> And everyone shall share i' th' gains.
> And now about the cauldron sing,
> Like neo-fascists in a ring,
> Enchanting all that you put in.   *Exit BANNON.*

SECOND WIDDECOMBE
  By the pricking of my thumbs,
  Something wicked this way comes.
  Hands off cocks,
  On with socks!   *Enter* BORIS JOHNSON.
BORIS JOHNSON
  How now, you secret, black, and midnight slags!
  What is't you do?
ALL
  A deed without a name.
BORIS JOHNSON
  A Michael Howard rim job? Tough crowd.
  I conjure you, by that which you profess,
  (Howe'er you come to know it) answer me:
  Though you may untie the economy
  Destroy the NHS. Exports stop,
  House building swallow, minorities taunt;
  Though turnips unharvest'd, and pigs bolt gunned;
  Though school roofs topple on their students' heads;
  Though royals prorogued and shit in rivers pumped
  Pure water turning brown; though the treasure
  Of Tories' germens tumble all together,
  E'en till destruction sicken, answer Bozzy
  To what he ask yous.
FIRST WIDDECOMBE
  Speak.
SECOND WIDDECOMBE
  Demand.
THIRD WIDDECOMBE
  We'll answer.
FIRST WIDDECOMBE

    Say, if thou'dst rather hear it from our mouths,
    Or from our masters?
BORIS JOHNSON
    Call 'em, let me see 'em.
FIRST WIDDECOMBE
    Pour in sow's blood, that hath been new
    Cull'd by Brexit; grease that's sweaten
    From some Covid cadavers throw
    Into the flame.
ALL
    Come, high or low;
    Thyself and office deftly show!
        Thunder. An APPARITION OF CHRIS PINCHER *rises.*
BORIS JOHNSON
    Speak, Pincher by name, Pincher by nature.
FIRST WIDDECOMBE
    He knows thy thought:
    Hear his speech, but say thou naught.
FIRST APPARITION
    Johnson! Johnson! Johnson! Beware the truth;
    Beware Sunak. And Truss. Dismiss me. Enough.
                                              Descends.
BORIS JOHNSON
    Whate'er thou art, for thy good pinchings, thanks;
    Thou hast harp'd my fear aright. But one word more.
FIRST WIDDECOMBE
    He will not be commanded. Here's another,
    More potent than the first.
        Thunder. An APPARITION OF EVGENY LEBEDEV *rises.*
SECOND APPARITION
    Boris! Boris! Boris!

BORIS JOHNSON
 Had I three ears, I'd hear thee.
SECOND APPARITION
 Your elbow is close. Yet you can't bite it.
 Be Bozzy brave and resolute. Laugh to scorn
 Attention seeking ministerial
 Resignations, for none who revelled hard
 Can harm Johnson. *Descends.*
BORIS JOHNSON
 Then lives Boris! For we were all at it!
 But yet I'll make assurance double sure,
 And take a bond of fate. I'll never quit;
 And endless shifting explanations give,
 About what I knew and when.
  Thunder. An APPARITION OF A CHILD CROWNED WITH
   A BORIS HAIRDO *rises.*
 What is this,
 That rises like the issue of the king,
 And wears upon his baby brow the round
 Blond mop of sovereignty?
ALL
 Listen, but speak not to't.
THIRD APPARITION
 Be bouffant-headed, proud, and take no care
 Who chafes, who frets, or where conspirers are:
 Johnson shall never vanquish'd be, until
 Chris Pincher quits and Michelle Donelan
 Does goes against him. *Descends.*
BORIS JOHNSON
 That will never be:
 I've ne'er heard of her! Who can bid a toff

Unfix his earth-bound right? Sweet bodements, good!
Rebellious Tories, rise never till
Class-ridden Britain fall, and our Johnson
Shall live the lease of fix'd-term parliaments,
Pay his dues to no one. And yet my heart
Throbs to know one thing: tell me, if your art
Can tell so much, shall Dom's subterfuge
Reinfect my reign?

ALL
Seek to know no more.

BORIS JOHNSON
I will be satisfied: deny me this,
And an eternal curse fall on you! Let me know.
Why sinks that cauldron? and what noise is this?

Music: Apache Indian, 'Boom Shak-a-Lak'.

FIRST WIDDECOMBE
Show!

SECOND WIDDECOMBE
Show!

THIRD WIDDECOMBE
Show!

ALL
Show his eyes, and grieve his heart;
Come like shadows, so depart!

A show of all JOHNSON's cheated-on partners carrying children appears, and pass over.

BORIS JOHNSON
Thou are too like the spirit of Carrie. Down!
Thy crown does sear mine eyeballs – and thy hair,
Thou other gold-bound brow, is Allegra.
A third is like Marina. – Filthy hags!

Why do you show me this? – A fourth! – Start, eyes!
What, will the line stretch out e'en to Arcuri?
Petronella! – A seventh! – I'll see no more: –
Yet Helen Macintyre appears. Who bears
A glass which shows many more; and I see
That twofold balls and treble children carry.
Horrible sight! Now I see 'tis true;
For the sprog-bolter'd women smile upon me,
And point at them for mine. What! is this so?

FIRST WIDDECOMBE

Ay, sir, all this is so: but why
Stands Johnson thus amazedly?
A man of your mind surely comprehends
The responsibilities of rearing bairns.
You wouldn't just get women pregnant and
Run. Would you? Come, we'll perform our antic
That this great liege may kindly say,
Our duties did his welcome pay.

Music. The WIDDECOMBES *dance, and vanish.*

BORIS JOHNSON

Where are they? Gone? Let this pernicious hour
Stand aye accursed in the calendar!
Come, some smoke-blowing lackey, goad my pride.

Enter NADINE DORRIES.

NADINE DORRIES

What's your majesty's will?

BORIS JOHNSON

Saw you the Widdecombes?

NADINE DORRIES

No, my lord.

BORIS JOHNSON

Came they not by you?
NADINE DORRIES
No, indeed, my lord.
BORIS JOHNSON
Infected be the air whereon they ride;
And damn'd all those that trust them! I did hear
The galloping of horse: is't Zahawi?
NADINE DORRIES
'Tis two or three more resignations sire
But I will ne'er desert you.
BORIS JOHNSON
More resignations? Cowards.
NADINE DORRIES
Ay, my good lord.
BORIS JOHNSON
Shills, they anticipat'st my exploit, while:
Their flighty instincts reflect upon our
Most shallow talent pool. No loss. From this time
The very first thought in my head shall be
The first thing of my hand. And even now,
To crown my thoughts with acts, be it so done:
The Cabinet I'll again reshuffle;
It's latest iteration; will blow minds.
My culture vulture Nadine, go and tell
Andrea Jenkyns and Brendan Clarke-Smith
That they're elevated to Cabinet.
I shuffle more than the house croupier.
But Boris come, no boasting like a fool;
This deed I'll do before this purpose cool:
Nads, massage my feet. Ashfield thence go I,
Where Lee Anderson's vanity, I'll ply.   *Exeunt.*

SCENE II

Enter JONATHAN GULLIS, MIRIAM CATES, NICK FLETCHER, BRENDAN CLARKE-SMITH.

MIRIAM CATES
Have you sent to Lee Anderson's house?
NICK FLETCHER
He cannot be heard of. His clinically vulnerable wife was
 self-isolating, while Boris invested in a wine fridge. Out of
 doubt he has withdrawn his support.
JONATHAN GULLIS
If he cedes his support over Partygate then our Nativist
 project is marr'd; it goes not forward, doth it?
MIRIAM CATES
It is not possible. You have not a man in all Ashfield able to
 rescue Boris but he.
JONATHAN GULLIS
No; he hath simply the best wit of any meat raffle veteran in
 Ashfield.
MIRIAM CATES
Yea, and the best looking too; and he is a very paramour for
 a working-class voice.
JONATHAN GULLIS
You must say 'paragon'. A paramour sounds like something a
 chai latte drinking Wokerati might drink.
           Enter ANDREA JENKYNS.
ANDREA JENKYNS
Masters, Graham Brady is coming from the '22; and there is
 fifty or sixty more colleagues more submitting no-
 confidence letters.

JONATHAN GULLIS
O sweet Lee Anderson! Thus could he have survived off thirty pence a day; he would have needed no more than thirty pence a day. And Boris had not given him thirty pence a day for supporting him, I'll be hanged. He would have deserved it: thirty p Lee, or nothing.

BRENDAN CLARKE-SMITH
Had Boris survived, we might have been made ministers. Instead, we'll lose our seats. *Enter LEE ANDERSON.*

LEE ANDERSON
Where are these Tories? Where are these hearts?

MIRIAM CATES
Lee! O most courageous day! O most happy hour!

LEE ANDERSON
Masters, I am to discourse wonders; but ask me not what; for if I tell you, I am not true Ashfieldian. I will tell you everything, right as it fell out.

MIRIAM CATES
Let us hear, sweet Lee.

LEE ANDERSON
Not a word of me. All that I will tell you is, Boris hath convinced me. He gets the public mood. He's very sorry. And he's going to invest in my constituency. Get your apparel together; blue rosettes to your suits, new ribbons to your pumps; meet presently at the palace; every Tory look o'er his part; for the short and the long is, Boris Johnson, by me, is preferred. In any case, let Gullis have clean linen; and let not him that fears strong female role-models, Nick, open his mouth in public, lest people think he's a simpering imbecile. Andrea is to become the Minister for Higher Education and Brendan, he's

promoted you to become a Parliamentary Under-Secretary of something or other. And, most dear Red Wallers, eat no onions nor garlic, for we are to utter sweet breath; and I do not doubt but to hear them say it is a sweet dislike of foreigners that sweeps the nation. No more words. Away, go, away! *Exeunt.*

SCENE III

Within Downing Street.
Enter with drum and colours, BORIS JOHNSON *and*
NADINE DORRIES.

BORIS JOHNSON
More resignations! What's wrong with these thanes?
What happened to the divine right of wangs?
Hang out my boxers onto Wilfred's swing;
E'en as more resign. My sycophants' strength
Will laugh this siege to scorn: let Doomsters wait
Till famine and STDs eat them up.
Were they not forc'd with those that should be mine,
I would have already fought, Blue on Blue,
And beat them backward home. *A cry of women within.*
What is that noise?
NADINE DORRIES
It is the cry of Carrie, my good lord.
BORIS JOHNSON
I have almost forgot the taste of beer.
The time has been, my drunken aides would be
The source of such a shriek; my fell of hair

Would at a joyful shindigs rouse and stir
As life were in't. I who supp'd full in lockdowns;
Hedonist, leader of boisterous japes,
Now by Confidence votes, from fun is barred.

Enter OLIVER DOWDEN.

Wherefore was that cry?

OLIVER DOWDEN
Dilyn, my lord, is dead.

BORIS JOHNSON
He should have died hereafter.
What cause?

OLIVER DOWDEN
Microwaved.

BORIS JOHNSON
My blood, like his, does boil.

NADINE DORRIES
A stupid dog. And perchance Carrie will
Realise what riches she has in you, now.

BORIS JOHNSON
What?

NADINE DORRIES
Four hundred watt, my sexy liege.

BORIS JOHNSON
Tomorrow, and tomorrow, and tomorrow,
Creeps on its petty paws from day to day,
To the last syllable of recorded time;
And all our microwaves have heated dogs
Their way to sizzling death. Out, out, brief Dilyn!
Life's but a walking shadow; a poor canine,
That cocks his leg on judges' feet at Crufts,
And then is heard no more: it is a tail

Told by an idiot, full of sound and fury,
Signifying nothing.   *Enter BRENDAN CLARKE-SMITH.*
Thou com'st to use thy tongue; No, not like that, Bren.
Thy story quickly.

BRENDAN CLARKE-SMITH
Gracious Boris,
I should report that which I say I saw,
But know not how to do't.

BORIS JOHNSON
Well, say, Bren.

BRENDAN CLARKE-SMITH
As I did watch upon yon GB News,
I looked upon Eamonn, and anon, he said,
Donelan has resigned.

BORIS JOHNSON
Liar, and slave!

BRENDAN CLARKE-SMITH
Let me endure your wrath, if't be not so.
Upon rolling news may you watch of it;
I say, Donelan's gone.

BORIS JOHNSON
If thou speak'st false,
Upon young Wilf's swing shall thou hang alive,
Till famine cling thee: if thy speech be sooth,
I care not if thou dost for me as much.
I pull in resolution; and begin
To doubt th' equivocation of those men,
That lie like truth. 'Fear not, till Donelan
Do hand in her notice'; Who even is
This Michelle Donelan? And why is she
Resigning? The game's up. My end is near.

There is nor flying hence nor tarrying here.
I 'gin to be aweary, I miss fun
And wish th' estate o' th' world were now undone.
Oh God, I sound like Dom! Blow, wind! come, wrack!
At least I'll go while still a silverback.

Enter MICHAEL GOVE.

MICHAEL GOVE
Turn, turn, Boris, turn!

BORIS JOHNSON
Oh Jon Bon Govi!
Of all men else I have avoided thee:
Go, get thee gak; my soul is too much charg'd
With plight of Vine already.

MICHAEL GOVE
I have no words;
My voice is in my leaked briefings: show me
Your moobs. So I may stab you in the front.

They wrestle, weakly.

BORIS JOHNSON
But Govester, tis you who losest labour:
As easy mayst one elevate Thirty P
To the deputy chair, as depose me:
Use thy famed treachery on someone else;
I bear a charmèd life, which must not yield
To one who partied also!

MICHAEL GOVE
Despair thy charm;
And let the fools whom thou still hast serv'd
Tell thee, Michael Gove during lockdown went
Cold Turkey!

ACT IV, SCENE III | 149

BORIS JOHNSON
Accursèd be that tongue that tells me so!
And be the gloomy Widdies no more believ'd,
That diddled with me in a double sense;
They kept the word of promise to our ear,
Then broke it to our hope!

MICHAEL GOVE
O imagine!
What sort of rogue would take a stick to the
Pinata of truth, breaking vows for sport?!

BORIS JOHNSON
Right then, you're dismissed for disloyalty.

MICHAEL GOVE
No. It is time to yield. The game is up.
You'll live to be the show and gaze o' th' time.
We'll have thee, as our rarer failures are,
Painted upon a pole, and underwrit,
'Here may you see the failed father of ten.'

BORIS JOHNSON
Eleven. Pah, no Gove shall outlast me.
Life is but a sport. And I will not yield
To kiss the ground before the bereaved's feet,
There to be baited with the rabble's curse.
Though Donelan did hand her notice in,
And thou oppos'd, did not in lockdown dance,
I will try to the last. Before my body
I'll call the Prime Minister's lectern forth:
And think of something to say on the spot!
Exeunt. Alarums. Retreat. Flourish. Enter, with drum and colours, GRAHAM BRADY, WILLIAM WRAGG *and*

the 1922 Committee, BRADY *carrying* JOHNSON's
papier mâché head on a plate.

GRAHAM BRADY

Hail, Tories! For so we art. Behold here
The partiers cursèd head. The time is free.
I see thee compassed with thy Party's best,
That speak my salutation in their minds,
Whose voices I desire aloud with mine:
Call: Leadership Election!

ALL

Call: Leadership Election! *Trumpets sound.*

GRAHAM BRADY

We shall not spend a large expense of time
Before we reckon with your several loves
Who Boris's successor is like to be,
Suella, Penny, Rishi, Kemi, Tom,
Jeremy, Nadhim or Liz, the next I
The chair of the 'Twenty Two gets to name,
Which would be planted newly with the time,
We need to get on with the jobs in hand –
Levelling up, crony contracts, tax fraud –
Delivered by our next Prime Minister
That unlike this tired reveller and's queen,
Who, as 'tis thought, by self and violent hands
Killed her own dog; won't waste eighty seats
And spaff our credibility's debris
On broken swings and fridges of white wine.
The membership will choose, by Thatcher's grace,
And we'll elect in measure, time, and place.
So, thanks to all at once and to each one,
Whom we invite to see next made head Con.

SCENE IV

Before Wembley Arena.
Enter two gentlemen, STEVE BAKER *and* MARK FRANCOIS.

STEVE BAKER
Mark, I haven't seen you for many moons.
MARK FRANCOIS
I was paintballing in Epping Forest. But now I'm back.
STEVE BAKER
After the hustings, our leadership election comes to an end this night.
MARK FRANCOIS
It is very near by this: Truss and Sunak are neck and neck.
STEVE BAKER
How many candidates have we lost in the action?
MARK FRANCOIS
Kemi Badenoch, Suella Braverman, Jeremy Hunt, Penny Mordaunt, Tom Tugendhat and Nadhim Zahawi all came up short.
STEVE BAKER
A victory is twice itself when the achiever brings home full numbers. I find here that Penny hath bestowed her honour on the young pork marketeer Truss.
MARK FRANCOIS
And equally remembered by Suella, who hath borne herself beyond the promise of her age, doing in the figure of a gerbil the feats of a griffin: she hath indeed better bettered expectation with her dreams of Kigali than you must expect of me to tell you how.

STEVE BAKER
  And what of Rishi?

MARK FRANCOIS
  Recommended by Jeremy Hunt only. There appears much hope in him. But not as much as in me. Andrew Bridgen has tipped us off about another silo of Brexit benefits not five miles hence.

STEVE BAKER
  Let's away, and find these benefits without delay. *Exeunt.*

SCENE V

Wembley Arena.
Enter a TV PRODUCER, LIZ TRUSS *and* THÉRÈSE COFFEY.

LIZ TRUSS
I pray you, is Simon Clarke here yet?

TV PRODUCER
Who?

THÉRÈSE COFFEY
Simon Clarke of Teesside, a once-in-a-generation thinker.

TV PRODUCER
He is returned, and the buffet in the green room is he hammering. Listen, Nick Ferrari and Rishi Sunak await your grace, we're live in three.

LIZ TRUSS
I only surround myself with brainy people. Simon promised to get me a wheel of Double Gloucester if I win. Pray you, do I look like Mrs Thatcher? I like headscarves. How many hath been killed in these Ukraine wars? I'm barred

ACT IV, SCENE V | 153

from Leeds Harvey Nichols for setting off the fire alarms. But it wasn't me.

TV PRODUCER
Faith, Liz, we're live in two; Nick Ferrari is ready to meet with you.

LIZ TRUSS
He's is a very valiant trencher-man; he hath an excellent stomach.

TV PRODUCER
And a good broadcaster, lady.

LIZ TRUSS
And a good broadcaster to a lady; but no Eamonn Holmes. I have a Kraft cheese slice here, a musty victual, pray, may I hath some help to unwrap it?

TV PRODUCER
We're going live, Liz, please step into the studio.

LIZ TRUSS
It is so; indeed, they're very complicated to open. You need a degree in astroturf physics! Well, we are all mortal.

Enter NICK FERRARI *and* RISHI SUNAK.

NICK FERRARI
Sack the girl in make-up. If it takes thirty minutes to this face improve, alternative employment she needs.

TV PRODUCER
And we're live in three, two, one.

NICK FERRARI
Good e'en to you and good cheer from the Wembley Arena, for the final hustings of this Conservative leadership election. There is a kind of merry war betwixt Rishi Sunak and Liz Truss; they never meet but there's a skirmish of wit between them. And tonight, we hope, members' minds

will be made. Good Liz Truss, Rishi Sunak you are to task
the membership to vote for you: please state your claims.

Music: Taylor Swift's 'Change'.

LIZ TRUSS
    What fire is in me! Coming from north Leeds,
    Condemned to attend the Roundhay School
    A leafy suburban hellscape true.
    Tis – after PPE at Merton – why
    I into politics got. To build change.
    No glory lives behind the back of such.
    But I were willing to the hard way go
    With photo shoots and lavish expenses.
    Dear Sunak: step down now, I oblige thee,
    Or else thy heart with sharpened mind I'll tame.
    If thou this aspiration nation lovs't
    Then bind our loves up by swift withdrawal.
    It's time to bring back British pride, and's why
    I invoke here, the Lionesses' spunk.
    In Liz we Truss. Put that on a bus.

NICK FERRARI
Thank you, Liz. You heard it full, Rishi: we may guess, from
    Liz, what a man you are. Truly the lady sells herself. Tell
    us, why should the Counties Home be ready for Rishi?

RISHI SUNAK
    Liz Truss's claims are proudly borne.
    She's a fantastic foreign secretary
    And the greatest advocate for cheese since
    That Babybell advert. 'Pause for laughs here.'
    My parents did strive for a better life
    Much sacrificing so I too could do

PPE – the condition of PMs.
With Graham Gooch, they daily, my spur are.
We hear now how many are censurèd:
'You cannot anything say more', 'tis true.
But to this nonsense woke, I will stand up.
With humility I will in kind lead.
For happy are they that can with grace hear
Their own detractions, and put them to mend.
In Rishi's heart is integrity pure
Lend me your vote and our pride I'll restore.

LIZ TRUSS
I wonder that you will still be talking, Sunak: nobody marks you.

RISHI SUNAK
My dear Liz Truss, I will fix the cost of living.

LIZ TRUSS
Well, I will fix the cost of, giving.

RISHI SUNAK
That makes no sense?

NICK FERRARI
Rishi. Liz. This is a zombie government and you've done nothing for these five weeks since.

LIZ TRUSS
Is it possible ambition should die while she hath such meet food to feed it as Richard Sunak?

RISHI SUNAK
Rishi.

LIZ TRUSS
Whatever, ambition itself must convert to apathy if you come in her presence.

RISHI SUNAK

I just think, people don't want to hear another tit-for-tat exchange. I set up the furlough scheme ...

LIZ TRUSS

Ludicrous left-wing nonsense. Richard ...

NICK FERRARI

Rishi.

LIZ TRUSS

Whatever, says we must speak tat instead of tit. I am an adult female human, with tits, not tats, despite what this *Guardian*-reading tofu-eating puberty-blocking ex-Chancellor wants me to have.

RISHI SUNAK

A Remainer was Liz, while a Brexiteer I always was.

LIZ TRUSS

Yes, a Remainer I used to be, and a Lib Dem, 'tis true. But now I believe in helping my moneyed backers pay less tax, and I don't think I've ever believed in anything harder.

Applause.

RISHI SUNAK

God keep your Ladyship in that mind; that some billionaires or other shall scape a predestinate taxing: On this we agree. *Applause.*

LIZ TRUSS

And I will grow our bond markets, and the pie, by halting the grave injustice of rich people paying into a collective, mutually beneficial pot.

RISHI SUNAK

Well, I am also pro-growth.

LIZ TRUSS

They will look on a tax-cutting budget of my hand more favourably, than a Marxist one of yours.

ACT IV, SCENE V | 157

RISHI SUNAK
I would my nineteen advisors had prepared me for debate of this strange sort, for I have much to say about modular house building on brownfield sites if there are ears to hear?

NICK FERRARI
I'm sorry, that is the sum of all, audience members, viewers at home, my dear friend Rupert Murdoch hath invited you all to watch of these adverts.

TV PRODUCER
Cut!

Enter THÉRÈSE COFFEY, SIMON CLARKE, DOMINIC RAAB.

LIZ TRUSS
Thérèse. How was I? If you swear, my lady, you shall not be forsworn.

THÉRÈSE COFFEY
I must make amends, for I was eating my pork pie.

SIMON CLARKE
Babe, you were fab.

LIZ TRUSS
Yes I was!

RISHI SUNAK
Please it you, Dom, how was young Rishi?

DOMINIC RAAB
You weak bastard. You came across like an overcoached droid. Liz for the masses spoke. In her awkward manner, spoke A-bombs of truth, which the nation will grow to love.

RISHI SUNAK
I thought you were for me?

DOMINIC RAAB
Should the hero of the evacuation of Kabul flatter, with simple watered judgement; or would you have me speak

after my style, as a professed no-holes-barred borderline sociopath?

RISHI SUNAK
I pray thee speak frothily.

DOMINIC RAAB
No. I' faith, methinks you're too low for a high praise, too brown for the membership, and too brittle for a great praise; only this commendation can I afford you, that were you other than you are, party members might like you. But being no other but you are, they do not.

RISHI SUNAK
I think'st you are in sport.

DOMINIC RAAB
Yes. Two hours on the Concept2 before breakfast. Fit body. Fit mind. *Exeunt.*

SCENE VI

LIZ TRUSS's victory party.
Enter LIZ TRUSS, JAKE BERRY, JACOB REES-MOGG, THÉRÈSE COFFEY and SIMON CLARKE.

LIZ TRUSS
The members' voice is clear! Run one before
And warn the Queen, t'other Liz nears her door.
Exit CLARKE.
Tomorrow,
Before the sun shall see's, I'll save the West
With a mini-budget. I thank you all,
Far-sighted were you, to side with Liz Truss!

Not as you served the cause, but as 't had been
Each yours like mine. You have shown stalwarts all.
Enter Downing Street. Tell your spouses, friends.
Tell them your feats, whilst they with joyful tears
Wash the woke elite from our nation state.
Let's face the global headwinds with proud grit,
And loose the potential of every Brit. *Exeunt.*

SCENE VII

A churchyard.
Enter two GRAVEDIGGERS *with spades.*

FIRST GRAVEDIGGER
Is she to be laid in state after she wilfully paid off that sex-trafficking victim who her son never met?

SECOND GRAVEDIGGER
I tell thee she is. There will be one queue for commoners and another queue for *Good Morning* presenters.

FIRST GRAVEDIGGER
A two-tier system, rigged in favour of the elite? That's a bit off-brand for the monarchy.

SECOND GRAVEDIGGER
Who cares? Tis *Good Mourning*. Do you think this new Prime Minister Truss was caught up in her demise?

FIRST GRAVEDIGGER
Ah, me. That woman. Correlation causation begets not, but here lies the point: if I meet Liz Truss wittingly, it argues exposure to a risk. If a four score and sixteen monarch is exposed, it argues the signing of a death warrant.

SECOND GRAVEDIGGER
Nay, but hear you, goodman delver ...

FIRST GRAVEDIGGER
Give me leave. Here lies our hole, which in this case is Balmoral; good. Here stands the Queen; good. If some lackey allows Liz Truss into the hole, it is, will she nill she, game over. Mark you that.

SECOND GRAVEDIGGER
Thus Truss, like our grave, is a black hole?

FIRST GRAVEDIGGER
Why there thou say'st: dense, and with an event horizon beyond which all perish. And the more pity that great folk should have countenance in this world to turbocharge us with meaningless banalities. Come, my spade. There is no ancient keyworker but gardeners, ditchers, and gravemakers: they hold up Kwarteng's profession.

SECOND GRAVEDIGGER
Was he a locksmith?

FIRST GRAVEDIGGER
Art thou deaf? Dost thou turn from the news? He's our chancellor. And his and Truss's mini-budget of £45 billion unfunded tax cuts hath caused the pound to collapse and government debt to soar. I'll put another question to thee. If thou answerest me not to the purpose, confess thyself.

SECOND GRAVEDIGGER
Go to.

FIRST GRAVEDIGGER
What is he that builds stronger than either the mason, the shipwright, or the carpenter?

SECOND GRAVEDIGGER
The Tory; for every one becomes a pier.

FIRST GRAVEDIGGER
I like thy wit well in good faith. Strong piers buffet the waves! But these Tories only do well to those that do ill and thou dost ill to say the Tories build well when they haven't built a single house in twelve years; argal. To't again, come.

SECOND GRAVEDIGGER
Who builds stronger than a mason, a shipwright, or a carpenter?

FIRST GRAVEDIGGER
Ay, tell me that, and unyoke.

SECOND GRAVEDIGGER
Marry, now I can tell.

FIRST GRAVEDIGGER
To't.

SECOND GRAVEDIGGER
Mass, I cannot tell.

FIRST GRAVEDIGGER
Cudgel thy brains no more about it, for your dull ass will not mend his pace with beating; and when you are asked this question next, say 'a grave-maker'. The houses he makes last till doomsday. Go; fetch me a stoup of liquor.

Exeunt.

SCENE VIII

At a Downing Street upper window.
Enter LIZ TRUSS and her maids aloft, SIMON CLARKE, THÉRÈSE COFFEY and SUELLA BRAVERMAN.

SIMON CLARKE
Braverman, Our Lady I do fret on,

Dumb, she stares into Boris's wine stains
Fidgeting with her Harvey-Nicks store card
As if her membership number embossèd
Were to be counted like rosary beads.

SUELLA BRAVERMAN
Be comforted, dear Simon.

SIMON CLARKE
No, I can not.
These peculiar, strange events keep on,
Mortgages rocket, and the market bedlam,
Proportioned to this cause, must be as great
As that it makes. Hush, she stirs.

LIZ TRUSS
Oh why me?
Betrayed by the Queen and the pound. Both dead.
The market's invisible hand hath raised
A white flag to our deep state Marxist foes
They cast their caps up and carouse together
Like friends long lost. The Bank of England buys
Government bonds; triple-turned Gove, Biden
The brokers, IMF and Global Left
Do conspire against us. Bid them all fly,
For when I am revenged upon this plot,
I have then done all. Oh my salad days.

Enter JAKE BERRY.

Has Kwasi gone?

JAKE BERRY
We field him out to graze.
His career's deader than Boris's marriage.
Look out o' th' other side of your window;
He slinks forth thither.

Enter, below the window, KWASI KWARTENG.

LIZ TRUSS

Oh, Kwasi Kwarteng!
The pound's dropped to a thirty-eight year low
I'm scrapping almost all of our tax cuts
O, Kwasi, Kwasi! Quit! You'll have to quit.

KWASI KWARTENG

Peace!
Not Truss's valour hath o'erthrown Kwasi,
But Kwasi's hath triumphed on itself.

LIZ TRUSS

Oh good, so it should be, that none but thee
Should conquer Kwasi, but woe 'tis so!

KWASI KWARTENG

Don't worry, I will go, Liz. I'll go. But
I here importune it awhile until
Of many thousand brave moves the poor last
The banker's bonus cap, you will still axe.

LIZ TRUSS

Dear Kwasi, pardon. I will try my best
For those brave boys. Not th' imperious show
Of the full-fortuned Deep State ever shall
Be brooched with me; while strife and chaos have
Edge, sting, and operation, I am safe.
Your life Chancellor, with its modest goal
Of fiscal mayhem, shall acquire no honour
Demurring upon me. But come, come, Kwasi –
Help him save his face – we must draw him up.
Assist, good friends.

KWASI KWARTENG

Yes please, the press waits. Brief me what to say.

COFFEY and CLARKE attempt to haul KWARTENG in through the window.

LIZ TRUSS
   Here's sport indeed! How heavy weighs my lord!
   Our strength is all gone into heaviness;
   That makes the weight. Had I great Bannon's power,
   The strong-winged NRA should fetch thee up
   And set thee by Trump's side. Yet you're too heavy;
   Wishers were ever fools. O well never mind,
              They give up the attempt to get KWARTENG *up through*
                                                      the window.
   It's not going to work. I'm afraid, friend,
   You'll just have to walk out Eleven's door,
   Like a crass unapologetic whore.
ALL
   A heavy sight.
KWASI KWARTENG
   OK. I am resignèd, Liz, I go.
   Give me some wine, and let me speak a little.
LIZ TRUSS
   No, let me speak, and let me rail so high
   That the false huswife Fortune break her wheel,
   Provoked by my offence.
KWASI KWARTENG
   One word, sweet queen:
   To the vile Deep State, take a bazooka.   *Phone beeps.*
KWASI KWARTENG
   The presser calls. I must to my end.   *Exit* KWARTENG.
SUELLA BRAVERMAN
   Right, let's talk about deportations, Liz.   TRUSS *stares.*
THÉRÈSE COFFEY
   She is dead too, our sovereign.

LIZ TRUSS
   I'm sorry, I was miles away, thinking
   By such poor passion as the farmer that
   Milks for supermarkets at a less than cost.
   All's but naught; It were more fitting for me
   To throw my red box at the injurious gods,
   And tell them that my world did equal theirs
   Till they had undermined my populist scheme.

SUELLA BRAVERMAN
   Liz. Like the illegals, you are at sea.
   And that you are so, I've just realised
   Our migration targets are not viable.
   Thus quit I too, in saying it's thy fault,
   I'll seem tough to morons. Therefore, goodbye.

                              Exit BRAVERMAN.
                              TRUSS stares.

JAKE BERRY
   Heavily moisturised Jeremy Hunt
   I'll switch for Kwasi Kwarteng's chancellor.
   And call Grant Shapps to replace Suella:
   He's always free. You two must rouse our queen.

SIMON CLARKE
   Madam?

THÉRÈSE COFFEY
   Madam, would you like a detox juice? Lady?

SIMON CLARKE
   Not even ginger, beets and dill stir her.

THÉRÈSE COFFEY
   Empress?

SIMON CLARKE
   O madam, madam, madam?

THÉRÈSE COFFEY
  In Liz we still Truss.

LIZ TRUSS
  Patience is sottish, and impatience does
  Become a dog that's mad. I'm no quitter
  To rush out of this house and simply quit
  Ere quitting come to us? No. How now, Thérèse?
  What, what! good cheer! Why, how now, Simon?
  My noble team! Ah, 'In Liz we Truss'! Look,
  Our lamp is spent, it's out! Good friends, take heart.
  It must be that energy crisis,
  We must strong remain, like the brave Black
    Knight
  In Monty Python's Holy Grail. 'It is
  But a scratch.' And so is Suella's loss.
  Come, away. We now have the fracking vote.
  Dress me like Thatcher, for we have no friend
  But resolution and the revolt's end.

SCENE IX

Outside a House of Commons toilet cubicle.

JAKE BERRY
  Thy oath remember; thou hast sworn to do't:
  'Tis but a blow, which never shall be known.
  Thou canst not do a thing in the world so soon,
  To yield thee so much profit. Let not conscience,
  Which is but cold, inflame in thy bosom
  The anti-fracking mandate you stood on.

ACT IV, SCENE IX | 167

Melt thee not: oppose Labour's amendment,
Save Liz. Be a soldier to our purpose.

ALEX STAFFORD

I will do't; because she is a goodly creature.

JAKE BERRY

The fitter, then, you vote against. Thou art resolved?

ALEX STAFFORD

I am resolved.

Exit BERRY.
Enter WENDY MORTON.

WENDY MORTON

I will use every leak, bribe, fraud and sext
To strew the no-lobby with Tory votes:
The Staffords, Fletchers, the Cates and the Wraggs,
Shall as a safety blanket protect Liz,
While lettuces do last. Ay me! poor whip,
Born to this tempest, a coldblooded whip,
This world to me is like a lasting storm,
Whipping me from my friends.

Toilet flushes. STAFFORD emerges from cubicle.

ALEX STAFFORD

Oh, Wendy, how now. Why are you in here?
I told Jake I'd vote no. But I think now
I might still vote yes after all. You see,
I campaigned on an anti-fracking stance
In Rother Valley. Lord, how your face just
Changed with this unprofitable news.
Come, let me past.

WENDY MORTON

No, I warn you;
You'll not bereave Liz Truss of your vote.

ALEX STAFFORD
  Come, come;
  I love Liz Truss our leader, and you too,
  With pure and backbench heart. We every day
  Hope she will defeat the mind virus woke.
  Our paragon though, by all reports fails:
  She is to repent the breadth of her cuts.
  Blame me for withdrawing my support. But
  I cannot support that which will frack me.
  Please, I beg you, be cheerful once again;
  And allow me to enter the lobby. Please?
WENDY MORTON
  Al, this could make life very tough for you.
  Think half an hour, Staffmeister, at the least:
  Think of what this will mean.
ALEX STAFFORD
  No, madam. Pray you get out of my way:
  Please, move kindly, do not heat your blood.
WENDY MORTON
  I just can't do that, Alex. [*Calls*] Guys. Back up.
              Enter JACOB REES-MOGG and THÉRÈSE COFFEY.
JACOB REES-MOGG
  Is the wind westerly that blows with the cold breath of
     Zephyrus?
ALEX STAFFORD
  It's the hand dryer.
THÉRÈSE COFFEY
  When I was born the wind was in the north.
JACOB REES-MOGG
  Kneel, weak Alex Stafford, and say your *actus contritionis*.

ALEX STAFFORD
    What?
THÉRÈSE COFFEY
    Your prayers. Say them.   *They seize* STAFFORD.
ALEX STAFFORD
    What mean you?
JACOB REES-MOGG
    If you do require some spaciousness for prayer, I Rees-
        Mogg, grant it:
    Pray; but be not tedious, for the Lord has strong,
        proficient ears.
    And we are sworn to do our noble Copernican work with
        haste.
ALEX STAFFORD
    You would make me vote?
THÉRÈSE COFFEY
    To satisfy Liz.
ALEX STAFFORD
    Why would she have me brought now?
THÉRÈSE COFFEY
    My commission
    Is not to reason the deed, but do it.
ALEX STAFFORD
    You will not do't for all the world, I hope.
    You are well favour'd, and your looks foreshow
    You have a gentle heart. I saw you lately
    Soothe Jonathan Gullis, who, headbutting
    A vending machine to release a Twix,
    Did concuss and bruise himself very hard.
    Good soothe, it show'd well in you: do so now:

Your lady seeks my vote; let you me go,
And save poor me, the weaker.

THÉRÈSE COFFEY
I am sworn,
Through the no-lobby
You will dispatch.

> REES-MOGG *and* COFFEY *seize him.*
> *Enter* CHRIS BRYANT *with phone camera drawn.*

CHRIS BRYANT
Hold, villains!

THÉRÈSE COFFEY
You goody-goody twat, Chris. Get thee hence.

CHRIS BRYANT
You're physically manhandling him.

ALEX STAFFORD
No they're not.

THÉRÈSE COFFEY
Yes we are.

JACOB REES-MOGG
Come, let us have this subversive reprobate abroad
suddenly.

> *Exeunt* REES-MOGG *and* COFFEY *with* STAFFORD.
> *Enter* CHARLES WALKER, *swigging from a pint of milk.*

CHARLES WALKER
These roguing crooks serve the dense pirate Truss;
And they have seizèd Stafford. Let him go:
There's no hope he'll return. I'll swear he'll cast
A ballot against's will. This shambles does
Taint us all, while at straws we feebly clutch
Her talentless tars does our great brand stain.
If Truss remains, at election we're slain.   *Exeunt.*

SCENE X

Downing Street.
Enter LIZ TRUSS, THÉRÈSE COFFEY *and* SIMON CLARKE.

LIZ TRUSS
  My desolation does begin to make
  A better life. 'Tis paltry to be Liz Truss;
  Not being Fortune, she's but Fortune's knave,
  A minister of her will.   *Flourish. Enter* OCADO DRIVER.
OCADO DRIVER
  Wow. Getting past SO15 was hard.
  My lady, we need to see the proof of
  Your order before I deliver here.
  Exactly valued, nothing admitted.
LIZ TRUSS
  Where's my unwanted new chancellor, Hunt?
                            Enter JEREMY HUNT.
JEREMY HUNT
  Here, madam.
LIZ TRUSS
  He's the new treasurer. Let him show you.
  And on his peril, that I have claimed naught
  On expenses. Speak the truth, Jeremy.
JEREMY HUNT
  Ma'am, I'd rather bankroll the NHS
  Than to my peril speak that which is not.
LIZ TRUSS
  You market-pleasing Judas. I've claimed what?
JEREMY HUNT
  Sufficient to make taxpayers see red.

Here's her food shopping order, and look at
This receipt for her inflight catering
While she was Foreign Secretary Truss.

Shows OCADO DRIVER.

OCADO DRIVER
Yeah, that's fine. I don't care, I'll leave it here.

Exit OCADO DRIVER.

THÉRÈSE COFFEY
Liz, blush not. We're Tories. We approve
Your wisdom in your deeds. And Jeremy's
A wanker. Always has been.

LIZ TRUSS
See, Thérèse!
How pomp is followed! Mine will be Rishi's
And when we shift estates, his would be mine.
The ingratitude of this Jeremy, who
I didn't want. O Hunt, of no more trust
Than those nice topless waiters I hired. Hence!
Or I shall show the cinders of my skills
Through th' ashes of our banks.

JEREMY HUNT
Sure. I will be next door if you need me.

Flourish. Exit HUNT.

LIZ TRUSS
He taunts me, girls, he taunts me, to make me
Be noble and quit. This will never chance.
I'll ne'er jump ere I'm pushed. I stuck it out
At Harrogate Safeway in ninety-three
Past the ton of spoiled kiwi fruit saga.
I can do it once more at Downing Street
And outface this our crashed bond market scene.

But hark thee, Simon Clarke.
>   *Whispers to* SIMON CLARKE.

SIMON CLARKE
　Good Liz, let me entreat you –
LIZ TRUSS
　No, Simon. What a wounding shame is this
　The anti-growth coalition have caused.
　Now daring our honour, the communist
　Stockbrokers, bankers and traders in gilt,
　Do reject the trickling down of our most
　Wonderful non-dom capitalist juice.
　The tofu-stainèd Linekerist mob
　Who think that paying seven hundred pounds
　More on their mortgages too great a price
　To ease the load on our poor billionaires!
　Make me U-turn my forty-five p cut
　Then demand they me my P forty-five.
　Addition of their envy! See, smoggy Stilts
　If you had tanked the markets, as a man,
　You would not have then lost the confidence
　Of this our Conservative Party.
　For women, different these conventions are.
　We may not market economies wreck
　Unreproved. Thus, I am now unfolded
　By conspiracies that will outlive me.
　Which smites me, beneath the fall I have.
>   *Enter* JAMES CLEVERLY.

JAMES CLEVERLY
　Where's this Liz?
THÉRÈSE COFFEY
　Behold, sir.

LIZ TRUSS
    James Cleverly.
JAMES CLEVERLY
    Madam, as thereto sworn by your command,
    I tell you this: Sunak through Brady
    Intends the leadership. Within six days
    You, sans dignity, will be sent before.
    Make your best use of this. I have performed
    Your pleasure and my promise.
LIZ TRUSS
    Suave Cleverly, is this how it all ends?
JAMES CLEVERLY
    Yes, Liz. May I loan your photographer
    To picture me posturing bravely in my office?
LIZ TRUSS
    I in your debt am James. Of course you may.
    Farewell, and thanks.
JAMES CLEVERLY
    Liz, adieu. Oh, and by the way did you
    Remember where you put the Trident codes?
LIZ TRUSS
    No, Jim, I didn't. Either they're in the
    Flagship L'Occitane shop on Regent's Street
    Or the Waitrose at Hop Oast services.
    Honestly, Jim, I'd forget my own head
    If it wasn't screwed on! I'm sure they'll be
    In the last place I look. That said, I've looked
    In lots of places for them for the last
    Time now. Still no luck. Like with that ice cube.
JAMES CLEVERLY
    I'd love to stay and chat, Liz, but I'm not

ACT IV, SCENE X | 175

Listening. Bye.   *Exit* CLEVERLY.

LIZ TRUSS
 Now, Thérèse, what think'st thou?
 Smooth Sunak shall be throned next week. And I
 An exotic puppet, like Roland Rat,
 Or green Orville, will be made to be shown
 As an example of what happens to
 True Conservatives who dare to stand up
 To the woke metropolitan elite.
 Mechanic serfs in greasy aprons shall
 Uplift us to the view. In their thick breaths,
 Rank of gross diet, shall we be enclouded,
 And forced to drink their Leftwaffe vapour.

SIMON CLARKE
 The gods forbid!

LIZ TRUSS
 Nay, 'tis most certain. Yoga instructors
 Will laugh and call us fools, Just Stop Oil will
 Our homes paint orange. Quick comedians
 Extemporally will stage us and present
 Our flea-bitten Downing Street failures; Liz
 Shall be brought useless forth, and I shall see
 Some squeaking Truss-alike pimp my greatness
 I' th' posture of a fool.

SIMON CLARKE
 O the good gods!

THÉRÈSE COFFEY
 Nay, that sounds pretty certain to be fair.

SIMON CLARKE
 I'll never see't, for I am sure mine nails
 Are stronger than mine eyes.   *A noise within.*

LIZ TRUSS
    Wherefore's this noise?
> *Enter WILLIAM WRAGG, removing a camera phone from his trousers.*

WILLIAM WRAGG
    Here's our rural kingmaker.
    That will not be denied your highness' presence.
    He brings you Toblerone.

LIZ TRUSS
    Let him come in.   *Exit WRAGG.*
    He brings me liberty.
    My resolution's placed, from head to foot
    I am marble-constant.   *Enter MICHAEL FABRICANT.*

LIZ TRUSS
    What? Michael? But what are you doing here?
    Where's Graham Brady, the kingmaker sure?

MICHAEL FABRICANT
    He's otherwise detained, ma'am. But fear not
    For tis I, Michael Fabricant, who am the
    Real power behind this the Tory throne.

LIZ TRUSS
    O Michael, hast thou brought a statement of
    My notice that, with Graham Brady, has
    Seen agreed a sentiment indulgent?

MICHAEL FABRICANT
Truly, I have it. But I have to remind you, I would not be the party that should desire you to sign it, for its signing is perpetual. Those that do sign of it, their careers seldom recover. Politically at least.

LIZ TRUSS
    These forty-four days feel like they've gone on
    A lifetime.

ACT IV, SCENE X | 177

MICHAEL FABRCIANT
Ah, yes, that has generally been the agreed experience of your tenure, madam.

LIZ TRUSS
Oh, Michael Fabricant. I am so scared.
What haps to Tory chiefs when their terms end?
What do they then do? Where do they then go?

MICHAEL FABRICANT
They go to the great lecture tour in the sky, ma'am. Or else they abide in rustic bliss in the Cotswolds. I heard of another one of them no longer than yesterday, a very honest man, but something given to lie; as a man should not do but in the way of honesty, how he now writes columns for the *Daily Mail* and does hundred grand a time speaking gigs in the US. Crucially, ma'am, in the Tory hereafter, so long as you refuse to repent, you will be entirely insulated from all the decisions you made as leader.

LIZ TRUSS
Oh, OK. Fine. Your basket. What's in it?

MICHAEL FABRICANT
'tis the pretty worm of Lichfield. One bite and your conscience is salved. I offer his services to all outgoing Tory prime ministers.

LIZ TRUSS
Why should Liz Truss's conscience relief need?

MICHAEL FABRICANT
I offer the worm without judgement, ma'am. The worm's an odd worm.

LIZ TRUSS
I see. You may leave the basket there.

MICHAEL FABRICANT
I wish you all joy of the worm.   *Sets down the basket.*

LIZ TRUSS
  Farewell.
MICHAEL FABRICANT
You must think this, look you, that the worm will do his kind.
LIZ TRUSS
  Ay, ay, farewell.
MICHAEL FABRICANT
Look you, the worm is not to be trusted but in the keeping of wise people; for indeed there is no goodness in the worm.
LIZ TRUSS
  Take thou no care; it shall be heeded.
MICHAEL FABRICANT
Very good. Give it nothing, I pray you, for it is not worth the feeding.
LIZ TRUSS
  Will it eat me?
MICHAEL FABRICANT
You must not think I am so simple but I know the devil himself would not eat Liz Truss, for fear of contracting stupid. 'Sides it didn't eat Dave or Theresa. And it only took a bite of Boris's bingo wings.
LIZ TRUSS
  Well, get thee gone. Farewell.
MICHAEL FABRICANT
Yes, forsooth. I wish you joy o' th' worm.   *Exit.*
          Re-enter THÉRÈSE COFFEY with a rail full of
                              fluorescent power suits.
LIZ TRUSS
  Give me my robes. Put out my lectern. I've

Immortal longings in me. Now, no more
The sap of Downing Street taps moist this lip.
> *CLARKE and COFFEY dress TRUSS as she scrolls her phone.*

Yare, yare, good Thérèse; quick. Methinks I hear
Good Donald call. I see him rouse himself
To praise my noble act. I hear him mock
The luck of Rishi, which the gods give him
To excuse wrath after. CPAC, I come!
Now to that brand my courage prove my title!
I am far right now; my other positions
I give my greener past. So, have you done?
Come then, I'll outside to face the MSM.
Farewell, kind Thérèse. Simon, long farewell.
> *Kisses them. CLARKE falls and faints.*

Have I this power in my lips? Dost fall?
If Stilts and nature can so gently part,
The force of Truss is even greater than
She dared think. Once more to the lectern, Liz.
'Tis just you and I now, sturdy Thérèse.
> *COFFEY's phone beeps.*

THÉRÈSE COFFEY
I'm afraid I've got to go away too,
In Rishi's new cabinet I am sought.
Bye. *Exit COFFEY.*

LIZ TRUSS
Now does this Emu lose her Rod Hull. Hence!
You chicken! Base abattoir volunteer.
I, to the acne scarrèd Bannon go.
His is my heaven to have. Oh you swine!
> *To the Worm of Lichfield, which she applies to her breast:*

With thy sharp teeth this mind intrinsicate
Of guilt at once untie. And venomous worm,
Hear: From small acorns Liz grows giant oaks.
Prime Minister from my bucket list is ticked.
Next on it: neo-fascist fantasist.
> *She steps outside into a barrage of camera flashes.*

ACT V

PROLOGUE

Enter CHORUS.

CHORUS
    Vouchsafe to those that have not read the story,
    That I may prompt them; and of such as have,
    I humbly pray them to admit the excuse
    Of time, of numbers, and due course of things,
    Which cannot in their huge and proper life
    Be here presented. Now bear we the tale
    To Kabul, Baghdad, Khartoum, Damascus;
    See there, junked translators, and forgotten
    Collaborators, friends of England once.
    Heave them away upon your winged thoughts
    Athwart the sea. Behold, the English beach
    Pales in the flood with thugs with flags and cans
    Whose jeers and shouts out-voice the deep-mouth'd sea,
    Which, as one racist mob, hates refugees
    A febrile spiteful mood, excited by
    Anderson, Jenrick, Braverman and Tice.
    You may imagine them leveraging –
    For naught more than personal advancement –
    The plight of those abandoned by the State
    That salted their earth, then tossed those who helped.
    And Rishi, ego bruised, and morals bent,

Still, from the hexèd chalice, keen to sup,
The billionaire's spouse's time has come.
And, free from scruples, and ambition fill'd;
He gives dog whistle, signal and ostent
To the brutes who hate on sight. Behold now,
In the quick forge and working-house of thought,
How far-right loons loose their attack hounds:
With economy tanked, health service choked,
Judicial grid lock and schools collapsèd
These crazed senators of disorder strut,
With riled plebians swarming at their heels,
Brazenly, for their own catastrophes,
Imputing refugees (and working poor)
For waiting lists, rents, prices and food banks.
Watch now these generals of violent discourse
Cravenly stoking the fears of the weak
And tabloid-blunted voters. Starmer too
Dreads headlines more than scruples, and plays at
Their dismal game. Now in London place us;
Where yet the lamentation of the sane
Begs all Conservatives to leave them be.
An election looms, the writing's wall'd, yet
Ere sanity reigns, there's two years more.
Now Sunak watch, his turn to take the reins.
Here must we bring him; and myself have play'd
The interim, by rememb'ring you 'tis past.
So brook abridgement, and your eyes pursue
After your thoughts, back to CCHQ.

SCENE I

CCHQ.
Flourish of cornets. Enter GRAHAM BRADY *with* RISHI SUNAK
and both their trains.

GRAHAM BRADY
  Dear Rishi, our next leader you shall be,
  We have dotted the i's and crossed the t's;
  Find keys to Number Ten in one of these:
                              To WILLIAM WRAGG:
  O, draw aside the curtains and discover
  The several caskets to our noble prince.
  Now make your choice.

RISHI SUNAK
  The first, of gold, who this inscription bears,
  'Who chooseth me shall gain what Conservatives desire.'
  The second, silver, which this promise carries,
  'Who chooseth me shall get what a Tory deserves.'
  This third, dull lead, with warning all as blunt,
  'Who chooseth me must give and hazard all he hath.'
  How shall I know if I do choose the right?

GRAHAM BRADY
  The one of them Rish, contains the keys.
  If you choose that, then the leadership's yours.

RISHI SUNAK
  Some aide direct my judgement! Let me see.
  I wish I could remember the end of
  Indiana Jones and the Last Crusade.
  What says this leaden casket?

'Who chooseth me must give and hazard all he hath.'
Must give, for what? For lead? Hazard for lead!
This casket threatens; Tories do not 'give'.
We take and take and take and take:
A golden mind stoops not to shows of dross,
I'll then nor give nor hazard aught for lead.
What says the silver with her elite hue?
'Who chooseth me shall get what a Tory deserves.'
As much as one deserves! Pause there, Sunakio,
And weigh thy value with an even hand.
If thou be'st rated by thy estimation
Thou dost deserve a lot, and yet a lot
May not extend so far as to Downing Street.
And yet to be afeard of my deserving
Were but a weak disabling of myself.
As much as I deserve! That's the leadership:
I do in birth deserve it, and in fortunes,
In graces, and in qualities of schooling;
But more than these, for patience I deserve,
In waiting for my turn while Liz fucked up.
Let's see once more this saying grav'd in gold:
'Who chooseth me shall gain what Conservatives desire.'
Why, that is power for its own proud sake,
From the four corners of the earth they come
To witness our prudent statesmanship.
The Qatari deserts and the vasty wilds
Of wide Arabia are as thoroughfares now
For sultans to come view our global brand.
The watery kingdom, e'en with the threat of
Rwanda at its end, is still no bar
To stop migrant boat people, who do come

As o'er a brook, seeking Tory rule.
One of these three contains the keys to Number Ten.
Is't like that lead contains them? 'Twere damnation
To think so base a thought. It were too gross
To rib such prestige in the obscure grave.
Or shall I think in silver they're immur'd
Being ten times undervalued to tried gold?
O sinful thought! Never so rich a gem
Was set in worse than gold. They have in England
A coin that bears the figure of King Charles Third
Stamped in gold; but his power's imagined;
Here lies real power in a golden bed
Lies all within. Deliver me the key.
Here do I choose, and thrive I as I may.

GRAHAM BRADY

There, take it, Rishi, if the keys are there,
Then they are yours.

He opens the golden casket. Inside a skull with a scroll in its eye.

RISHI SUNAK

O hell! what have we here?
A carrion Death, within whose empty eye
There is a written scroll. I'll read the writing.
All that glisters is not gold,
Often have you heard that told.
Many a Brexit hath been sold
Sunlit Uplands to behold.
But gilded tombs worms infold.
Had you been as wise as bold,
Young in limbs, in judgement old,
Your answer had not been inscroll'd,

Fare you well, your bid is cold.
Cold indeed and labour lost,
Then farewell keys, and welcome frost.
Brady, adieu! I have too griev'd a heart
To take a tedious leave. Thus losers part.

Flourish of cornets.

GRAHAM BRADY
Not so fast, Rishi, this was all for show.
We're out of choices, just have the keys.
Go! *Exeunt.*

SCENE II

Junction 28 of the M1 in South Normanton.
Enter JONATHAN GULLIS, LEE ANDERSON, MIRIAM CATES,
NICK FLETCHER, BRENDAN CLARKE-SMITH, MARK
JENKINSON and ANDREA JENKYNS.

LEE ANDERSON
Are we all met?

MIRIAM CATES
Pat, pat; and here, at the Holiday Inn at junction 28 of the M1 in South Normanton, is a marvellous convenient place for a meeting of the Red Wall's greatest minds. This Monster-can and condom-strewn car park shall be our stage, this fag-end-covered picnic bench our tiring-house; and we will discuss our course of action, as we will do it before the nation.

LEE ANDERSON
Miriam Cates.

MIRIAM CATES
What sayest thou, Lee Anderson?
LEE ANDERSON
There are things in this manifesto of ours that will never please. First, as Nigel Farage keeps pointing out, illegals pour into this country by small boat. Yet nowhere in it does it say that we will spend billions of pounds deporting them to Rwanda. Which is what the public want. How answer you that?
NICK FLETCHER
By'r lakin, a parlous fear.
BRENDAN CLARKE-SMITH
Maybe we must abandon the Stop the Boats rhetoric, when all is done?
LEE ANDERSON
Don't be absurd; I have a device to make all well. Let's just do it anyway, and pretend our manifesto said we will Stop the Boats, when it said no such thing, and that our mandate is for that indeed; and for the more better assurance, tell them that I Lee Anderson am not Lee Anderson from old Labour, but Lee Anderson from the New Conservatives. This will put them out of all fear.
MIRIAM CATES
Well, we will have work from this imaginary manifesto; and it shall be written in sixteen-point Arial.
LEE ANDERSON
No, make it twenty. And let it be written in Comic Sans.
NICK FLETCHER
Will not the ladies be afeard of dehumanised foreigners?
JONATHAN GULLIS
I fear them, I promise you.

LEE ANDERSON

Masters, you ought to consider with yourselves, to bring in (God shield us!) illegals among ladies is a most dreadful thing. For there is not a more fearful threat than a rabid illegal migrant living; and we ought to leverage that.

NICK FLETCHER

Therefore another manifesto must also state that strong male-role models like James Bond must not be replaced by women, as has already happened with *Doctor Who*, *Ghostbusters* and Luke Skywalker.

MIRIAM CATES

Not now, Nick.

NICK FLETCHER

The Equalizer ...

MIRIAM CATES

Shut him up.

LEE ANDERSON

No, we must be seen to state thus, or to the same defect: 'A up, ladies,' or, 'A up, fair ladies, I would wish you,' or, 'I would request you,' or, 'I would entreat you, not to fear, not to tremble: my life for yours. If you think that we would let illegals come here to murder, pillage, rape and fly tip it were pity of my life. No, we will do no such thing; we will vilify them, as the press barons would, to distract from their looting: and once we have exhausted all the political capital we can from these desperate souls, deport them to Kigali.'

MIRIAM CATES

Yes, it shall be so. But there is two hard things: that is, to get this done now we're on the fifth Prime Minister since two thousand and ten.

LEE ANDERSON
Simples. We'll just say 'fuck off back to France'.
MIRIAM CATES
And then there is another thing: we must keep the Red Wall in the great chamber. For we are polling dreadfully, and our continuing ability to dictate the agenda relies on it entirely.
BRENDAN CLARKE-SMITH
We must defend the wall. What say you, Lee?
LEE ANDERSON
Some man or other must singlehandedly present for the Red Wall. And let him speak for the entire working class of the area that signifies Red Wall. And let him hold his fingers thus, and through that cranny shall immigrants be told to get stuffed.
MIRIAM CATES
If that may be, then all is well. Come, sit down, every mother's moron, and let's rehearse my party-political broadcast. Lee, you begin: when you have spoken your speech, go to your GB News slot; and so everyone according to his briefing.
Enter ISABEL OAKESHOTT *behind.*
ISABEL OAKESHOTT
What hempen homespuns have we swaggering here,
So near the cradle of my Ticey Queen?
What, a play toward? I'll be an auditor;
An actor too perhaps, if I see cause.
MIRIAM CATES
Speak, Lee. Gullis, stand forth.
LEE ANDERSON
Jonathan, the foreigners of Albania have odious vile …

MIRIAM CATES
    Odours, odours.

LEE ANDERSON
    ... odours vile
    So hath thy breath, my dearest Gullis dear.
    But hark, a voice! Stay thou but here awhile,
    And then I will on GB News appear. *Exit.*

ISABEL OAKESHOTT
    A better Anderson than e'er played here! *Exit.*

JONATHAN GULLIS
Must I speak now?

MIRIAM CATES
Ay, marry, must you, for you must understand he goes but to make a noise on a conspiracy-theory-propagating TV station part owned by a company based in Dubai, and is to come again.

JONATHAN GULLIS
    Most radiant Great Britain, most red, white and blue,
    Of colour like wine on LuLu Lytle chaise long,
    Most lusty Island folk, who for NHS queue,
    I'm true as Yorkshire Water sewage discharge pong,
    I'll meet thee, Anderson, at Albania.

MIRIAM CATES
Albion man, Albion! Why you must not speak that yet, you speak all your part at once, cues and all. Lee, come back here, let's marginalise trans people.

    Enter ISABEL OAKESHOTT *and* LEE ANDERSON *with an ass's head and Reform UK rosette.*

LEE ANDERSON
If I were fair, Gullis, I were only thine.

ACT V, SCENE II | 191

MIRIAM CATES
O monstrous! O strange! We are haunted. Pray, masters, fly, masters! Help! *Exeunt Clowns.*

ISABEL OAKESHOTT
I'll ghost write you. I'll lead you about a round,
Through bog, through bush, through brake, through brier;
Sometime a hack I'll be, sometime a hound,
A pen, a blogging horse, sometime a liar;
And crow, and bark, and neigh, and spit, and burn,
Like hack, hound, horse, skank, scribe, at every turn.
Exit.

LEE ANDERSON
Why do they run away? This is a knavery of them to make me afeard. *Enter NICK FLETCHER.*

NICK FLETCHER
O Lee, thou art changed! I wish I had a strong male role model to refer to right now. What do I see on thee?

LEE ANDERSON
What do you see? You see an ass-head of your own, do you?
Exit FLETCHER.
Enter MIRIAM CATES.

MIRIAM CATES
Bless thee, Lee! bless thee! Thou art translated. *Exit.*

LEE ANDERSON
Translated? Urgh. I only speak English. I see their knavery. This is to make an ass of me, to fright me, with imaginary threats. But I will not stir from this place, do what they can. I will walk up and down here, and I will sing, that they shall hear I am not afraid. *Sings:*
The Ashfield cock, so pink of hue,
With Asda-stylish twill,

The miner with scapegoats so true,
The git with grievance shrill.

TICEANIA *Waking.*
What angel wakes me from my flowery bed?

LEE ANDERSON *Sings:*
The poor, the migrant, and the cheat,
The plain-song British bloke,
Whose note full many a man doth greet,
And dares not answer, 'woke'.
For, indeed, who would set his wit to so overlooked a man? Who would give an indigenous Brit the lie, when he cry 'woke' never so?

TICEANIA
I pray thee, gentle pit scab, sing again.
Mine ear is much enamour'd of thy note.
So is mine eye enthrallèd to thy bulk;
And thy fair boarish force perforce doth move me,
On the first view, to say, to swear, I love thee.

LEE ANDERSON
Methinks, Richard, you should have little reason for that. You're a pound-shop Farage. And yet, to say the truth, reason and love keep little company together nowadays. The more the pity that some honest, native neighbours will not make them friends.

TICEANIA
Thou art as wise as thou art beautiful.
Come into this Holiday Inn with me.

LEE ANDERSON
Not so, neither; but if I had wit enough to stop all immigration, I have enough to serve mine own turn. Bye.

ACT V, SCENE II | 193

TICEANIA
　Out of Reform do not desire to go.
　Thou shalt remain here whether thou wilt or no.
　I am a tycoon of no common rate.
　Pure Sterling still doth tend upon my state;
　And I do want thee: therefore, go with me.
　I'll give thee fairies to attend on thee;
　And they shall fetch thee pasties from the Greggs,
　And beer, while thou on Holiday Inn sheets sleep.
　And I will purge thy Tory grossness so
　That thou shalt like a Reform spirit be. –
　Mummery! Habib! Bull! and Lance Forman!
　　　　　　　　　　　　　　Enter four Fairies.

BEN HABIB
　Ready.
JUNE MUMMERY
　And I.
DAVID BULL
　And I.
LANCE FORMAN
　And I.
ALL
　Where shall we go?
TICEANIA
　Be kind and courteous to this Northerner;
　Hop in his walks and gambol in his ears;
　Feed him with pork scratchings and Madri beers,
　With Seabrook crisps, Cheese Strings, Double-Deckers;
　Give money-bags stole from Exchequers,
　And a sweetener, a huge SUV,

A monstrosity, at six MPG,
To help him drive to work, and stay blunt;
Go, pluck policy from the National Front
Nod to him, elves, and do perform this stunt.
And fan the hubris of this Ashfield ...

JUNE MUMMERY
Hail, mortal!

BEN HABIB
Hail!

DAVID BULL
Hail!

LANCE FORMAN
Hail!

LEE ANDERSON
I cry your worships mercy, heartily. I beseech your worships' name.

BEN HABIB
Habib.

LEE ANDERSON
I shall desire you of more acquaintance, good Master Habib. If I mess up in an interview, I shall make bold with you. Your name, honest fisherwoman?

JUNE MUMMERY
Mummery.

LEE ANDERSON
I pray you, commend me to 'Mum', your mother, and to 'Mery', your father. Good Mistress Mummery, I shall desire you of more acquaintance too. Your name, I beseech you, sir?

DAVID BULL
Dr David Bull.

LEE ANDERSON
Good Doctor David Bull, I know your patients well. That
  same cowardly Talk TV are idiots for axing your Weekend
  Breakfast Show. I promise you, your Perma-tanned
  presenting style hath made my eyes water ere now. I desire
  you of more acquaintance, good Doctor David Bull.

TICEANIA
Come, wait on him. Lee, defect, join our story.
Sunak, methinks, look with a jealous eye,
And when he weeps, weeps every little Tory,
Lamenting their enforcèd probity.
Tie up my love's tongue, bring him silently.

SCENE III

A grouse moor in Richmond.
Enter GREG HANDS *carrying shotguns, and cartridges with
letters in them. With him* SUELLA BRAVERMAN, OLIVER
DOWDEN, PENNY MORDAUNT, MICHELLE DONELAN, RISHI
SUNAK, MICHAEL GOVE, JEREMY HUNT, GRANT SHAPPS, *and
others, with bows.*

GREG HANDS
Come, Rishi, come. Penny, this is the way.
Grant Shapps, let me see your precision.
Be you remembered, our star Lee's gone, Lee's fled.
So, fellow Tories I've organised this
Team-building excursion to morale raise.
Happily we may blast grouse from the sky
And work out how to proceed now our star's gone.

First; Jeremy and Michael Gove, you must do this;
'Tis you must dig with mattock and with spade,
And pierce the inmost centre of the earth:
Then, when you come to Pluto's region,
I pray you, deliver him this petition;
Tell him, it is the note Labour left us
And that it says that 'there's no money left'!
And that it comes with regret from Greg Hands
Shaken with sorrows by ungrateful Lee.
This wicked Ticeania, my sidekick's nicked;
Come, Tories, now we must go tout for justice.

OLIVER DOWDEN
O Rishi, is this not a heavy case,
To see this ex-Chairman thus distracted?

RISHI SUNAK
Yes, so my friend, my ace strategy is
By day and night attend him carefully,
And feed his humour kindly as we may,
While keeping his mania from the press.

SUELLA BRAVERMAN
Weak men, his sorrows are past remedy,
Lee was Box Office but let's not lament.
With these hate marches in town, we must vent.

RISHI SUNAK
Please, no more venting without Rishi's seal.

GREG HANDS
Jeremy, how now? How now, my masters?
What, have you met with Lee?

JEREMY HUNT
No, my good lord; but Pluto sends you word,
If you will have Revenge from hell, you shall.
For Justice, is now in heaven with Jove

And in its gridlock stuck, since Grayling's cuts,
So that perforce you must needs stay the time.
GREG HANDS
He doth me wrong to feed me with delays.
I'll dive into the burning lake below,
And pull Lee out of Reform by the heels.
Come, to this gear. You are a good marksman, Penny.
He gives them shotgun cartridges.
'Ad Thatcher,' that's for you; here, 'Ad Enoch
 Powell';
'Ad Reagan,' that's for myself;
Here, boy, 'to Scruton'; here, 'to Rush Limbaugh';
'To Mosely,' Olly, not to Ian Paisley;
You were as good to shoot against the wind.
To it, boy. – Rishi, shoot when I bid. –
Of my word, I have written to effect;
There's not a god left unsolicited.
RISHI SUNAK
Kinsmen, shoot all your guns into the sky.
We'll humour poor Greg, keep's mind occupied.
GREG HANDS
Now, masters, fire. *They shoot.*
O Rishi, well, well said!
Good boy, in Oswald's lap! Give it Rishi.
Lords, 'there's no money left', none left I say,
Read on the mess that Labour did leave us!
SUELLA BRAVERMAN
My lord, I aim a mile beyond the moon.
Your letter is with Pinochet by this.
MICHAEL GOVE
I think it was a peregrine in truth.

GREG HANDS
> Ha! ha! Suella, Suella, what hast thou done?
> See, see, thou hast shot off one of Thatcher's horns.

OLIVER DOWDEN
> This was the sport, my lord; when Suella shot,
> Thatcher, being galled, gave Mosely such a knock
> That down fell one of his brown shirts in court;
> And who should find it but that Enoch Powell?
> He laughed, and told Oswald he should not choose
> But give it Anderson for a present.

GREG HANDS
> Why, there it goes. God give his lordship joy!
>> *Enter* DESMOND SWAYNE *with a basket and two pigeons in it.*
>
> News, news from heaven! Olly, the post is come.
> Sirrah, what tidings? Have you any letters?
> Shall I have justice? What says the Iron Lady?

DESMOND SWAYNE
> Ho, the gibbet-maker? She says that she hath taken them
> down again, for no Just Stop Oil eco-Nazis can be hanged
> till the next week at least.

GREG HANDS
> But what says Mrs Thatcher, I ask thee?

DESMOND SWAYNE
> What are you talking about? She is dead; I never spoke with
> her in fifteen years.

OLIVER DOWDEN
> Psst, Des, psst, Des, Psst, Des, psst, Des, psst. Des.
> We're doing positive affirmation.
> Greg has lost the plot, so we're unloading
> That Labour note they left us at the sky,
> And so are vainly hoping remedy

Presenteth itself, 'ere we're called to act.
DESMOND SWAYNE
Positive what? Is this what the party has come to? I always knew you were bent, Dowden. I'll have none of your woke psychobabble. Where's that new twat Rishi? Are you allowing all this?
RISHI SUNAK
The plan is working.
GREG HANDS
Why, villain, art not thou the carrier?
DESMOND SWAYNE
Ay, of my pigeons, Greg; nothing else. You'll get no woke affirmation from me.
GREG HANDS
Why, didst thou not come from heaven?
DESMOND SWAYNE
From heaven? Almost, the New Forest. Why, I am going with my new pigeons to an ERG meeting. Steve Baker thinks he's found some Brexit dividends.
GREG HANDS
Sirrah, come hither. Make no more ado,
But give your pigeons to Lee Anderson.
Beg him to return, without him we're lost.
Hold, hold; meanwhile here's money for thy charges.
Give me pen and ink.
Sirrah, can you with a grace deliver up a supplication?
DESMOND SWAYNE
Ay, sir. Lee is a man after my own heart.
GREG HANDS
Then here is a supplication for you. And when you come to him, at the first approach you must kneel; then kiss his foot; then deliver up your pigeons; and then wait

for him to say 'yes'. I'll be at hand, Des; see you do it
bravely.

DESMOND SWAYNE
I warrant you, Greg; let me alone. I'm not kissing Lee's feet
though.

GREG HANDS
Knock at my door, and tell me what he says.

DESMOND SWAYNE
God be with you, sir; I will.   *Exit.*

GREG HANDS
Come, Tories, let us go.   *Exeunt.*

SCENE IV

TICEANIA
Come, sit on my budget hotel bed,
While I thy hubristic cheeks do coy,
And stick blank cheques in thy sleek smooth hand,
And kiss thy fair large ears, my gentle joy.

LEE ANDERSON
Where's Dr David Bull?

DAVID BULL
Ready.

LEE ANDERSON
Scratch my head, David. Where's Monsieur Forman?

LANCE FORMAN
Ready.

LEE ANDERSON
Monsieur Forman; good monsieur, get you your weapons in
your hand and spear me an Atlantic salmon in a shit-filled

ACT V, SCENE IV | 201

river; and, good monsieur, smoke it. Do not fret yourself too much in the action, monsieur; and, good monsieur, have a care you smoke it well; I would be loath to have your evident far-reaching political expertise embarrassed by a bad smoking, signor. Where's Mademoiselle Mummery?

JUNE MUMMERY
Ready.

LEE ANDERSON
Give me your neaf, Madam Mummery. Pray you, leave your courtesy, good madam.

JUNE MUMMERY
What's your will?

LEE ANDERSON
Nothing, good madame, but to help Dr David Bull to scratch. I must to the Ashfield barber's, madame, for methinks I am marvellous hairy about the face; and I am such a tender ass, if my hair do but tickle me, I must scratch.

TICEANIA
What, wilt thou hear some music, my sweet love?

LEE ANDERSON
I have a reasonable good ear in music. Let us have some Bell and Spurling.

TICEANIA
Or say, sweet love, what thou desirest to eat.

LEE ANDERSON
Truly, a peck of advacados; I could munch some good animal feed. Methinks I have a great desire to a bottle of silage.

TICEANIA
I have a venturous fairy that shall seek

The Brexit hoard, sovereignty's fruits.
LEE ANDERSON
I had rather have a can or two of mushy peas. But, I pray you, let none of your people stir me; I have an exposition of bigotry come upon me.
TICEANIA
Sleep thou, and I will wind thee in my arms.
Candidates, go your incoherent ways.
So I'll Anderson my sweet imbecile
Gently entwist, the race-baiter will
Enring the climate crisis denier.
O, how I love thee! How I dote on thee! *They sleep.*

SCENE V

Chipping Norton.
Enter RISHI SUNAK and OLIVER DOWDEN.

RISHI SUNAK
O grave and good Suella, the great comfort
That I did have of thee!
OLIVER DOWDEN
Scourge of the imaginary hate march
Suella Braverman? Forget her, sir.
She's a poisoned malice, sovereign sir.
And since that you have kindly vouchsafed, sir,
Since Suella's sacking, to ask my guidance.
It is a surplus of your grace which never
My life may last to answer, sir. Lest you
Might like to promote me.

ACT V, SCENE V | 203

RISHI SUNAK
  O Oliver,
  We honour you with trouble. But I came
  To see the cabin of Dave Cameron
  This glamping site we've pass'd through, but seen not
  The accidental Brexit architect.

OLIVER DOWDEN
  As he reigned peerless,
  So his Shepherd's Hut, I do well believe,
  Excels whatever yet you look'd upon
  Or hand of man hath done; therefore they keep it
  Lonely, apart. But here it is: prepare
  To see a world beating getaway space.

They discover DAVID CAMERON'S
Shepherd's Hut.

  I like your silence, it the more shows off
  Your wonder: but yet speak?

RISHI SUNAK
  It's natural posture!
  A classic design, curved roof, cast iron wheels,
  An idyllic hideaway, perfect lair
  With decorative ironmongery
  But yet, Oliver, this hut looks brand new.

OLIVER DOWDEN
  So much the more Cameron's excellence,
  Which can live here some eight years without scratch.
  Music, awake Dave: strike!

Music: Celine Dion, 'My Heart
Will Go On'.

  'Tis time; descend; be lone no more; approach;
  Strike all that look upon with marvel. Come;

I'll ope' your hut up: stir; and come away.
Bequeath to us your talent, for from here
Rishi redeems you. You perceive he stirs.

Lord CAMERON *of Chipping Norton emerges from his Shepherd's Hut. Embracing* CAMERON.

RISHI SUNAK
O, he's warm!
And so become our electoral hopes.
If this be magic, let it be an art
Lawful as eating.

OLIVER DOWDEN
That he is living
Here, were it told you, should be hooted at
Like an old tale; but here does David live,
Though yet he speak not. Mark a little while.
Please you to interpose, fair Rishi. Kneel
And say a Hindu mantra. Turn, David,
Your next job move is found.

SUNAK kneels before CAMERON.

RISHI SUNAK
Om. Earth, Sky, Heaven
We meditate on the
Brilliant light of the Sun:
May it illuminate our minds!
Lord Cameron, please will you be
Rishi Sunak's foreign secretary?

DAVID CAMERON
Your gods, look down,
And from their sacred vials pour their graces
On Rishi Sunak's head! Of course, Dave will.

Life's boring. I miss frontline politics.
There's limited times you can supper with
The Clarksons before the mind rot sets in.
Tell me, mine heir, what new problems we face?
Is Brexit ignored, do we exploit race?

OLIVER DOWDEN

There's time enough for that; Go together,
Us precious winners all; our exultation
Partake to everyone. I, an odd turtle,
Will wing me to some wither'd bough, and there
Ere a more senior cabinet role
Is proposed, lament until I am lost …

RISHI SUNAK

Peace, Oliver!
Thou shouldst Deputy take by my consent,
As I by thine have rediscovered Dave,
He's Electoral catnip to those dull
Citizens whose memories do not work.
This respectable Foreign Minister
Will take them by the hand, whose poverty
Is richly noted, and here justify
That only voting for more of the same,
Will make this England rich again. Olly,
Lead us from hence; where we may leisurely
Each one demand, and answer to his part
Perform'd in this wide gap of time, since first
We were dissever'd. Hastily lead away.

SCENE VI

A hotel housing asylum seekers in London.
Enter NIGEL FARAGE, TOMMY ROBINSON, RIOTERS
and POLICE.

NIGEL FARAGE
He that will not see Turks stealing their jobs, Somalians stealing their houses, and Albanians stealing their futures, list to me.

FIRST RIOTER
It will come to that pass, if strangers be suffered. Mark him.

SECOND RIOTER
Suella said we were being invaded the other day, and she can't be lying because she's always on the TV.

NIGEL FARAGE
Our country is a great country; ergo –

TOMMY ROBINSON
Asylum seekers are nonces?

RIOTERS
Yes!

THIRD RIOTER
They bring in strange foods too, which is to the undoing of us locals; for what's a Halal to a good British chip?

SECOND RIOTER
Trash, trash; they breed sore eyes, and tis enough to infect the city with the palsey.

TOMMY ROBINSON
Nay, it has infected it with the palsey; for these bastards of dung, as you know they grow in dung, have infected us,

ACT V, SCENE VI | 207

and it is our infection will make the city shake, which partly comes through the eating of Halal.

POLICE SERGEANT
You are causing a large-scale disturbance. We have enacted a dispersal order. Please leave the area.

TOMMY ROBINSON
You would have us upon this, would you? They're paedophile protectors!

RIOTERS
Paedophile protectors! *Exit FARAGE quietly.*

POLICE SERGEANT
Step back, sir.

TOMMY ROBINSON
I bow to nobody bar the king and my coke dealer. We will show no mercy upon the strangers.

RIOTERS
Tommy, Tommy, Tommy!

POLICE SERGEANT
You are the simplest things that ever stood.

TOMMY ROBINSON
How say ye now, patriots? Patriots simple! Down with him!

RIOTERS
Patriots simple! patriots simple!
They move on the POLICE line.
Enter SADIQ KHAN.

SADIQ KHAN
   Hold! in TFL's name, hold!

TOMMY ROBINSON
Scum, you hate this country!

ALL
Scum!

SADIQ KHAN
　Peace, how, peace! I charge you, keep the peace!
FIRST RIOTER
It's Sadiq! He wants to turn Haringey into a Caliphate!
SECOND RIOTER
He's trying to Sharia law us!
THIRD RIOTER
Let's hear him: My brother, Arthur Watchins, cycles to work and he says Sadiq's traffic-calming measures have been quite helpful. Let's hear Sadiq Khan.
SECOND RIOTER
I bet your brother runs red lights.
FIRST RIOTER
And cuts up HGVs.
SADIQ KHAN
　Even by the rule you have among yourselves,
　Command still audience.
SECOND RIOTER
Lee Anderson says you're in the pocket of Islamists. And Lee's normal, like us.
ALL
Sadiq Khant!
SADIQ KHAN
　You that have voice and credit with the number
　Command them to a stillness.
TOMMY ROBINSON
No way, you Jihadi traitor. I'm a proud Englishman. If I did that I may as well be a Muslamic Halalist.
SADIQ KHAN
　Then what a rough and riotous charge have you,
　To lead those that Tommy cannot rule?

ACT V, SCENE VI | 209

Good masters, hear me speak.

THIRD RIOTER
Aye, by th' mass, we should, More: th' art a fair to average administrator, and I thank thy good worship for my brother Arthur Watchins.

Enter a POLICE water cannon.

ALL
Peace, peace.

SADIQ KHAN
Look, what you do offend you cry upon,
That is, the peace: not one of you here present,
Had there such fellows lived when you were babes,
That could have topped the peace, as now you would,
The peace wherein you have till now grown up
Had been ta'en from you, and the bloody times
Could not have brought you to the state of men.
Alas, poor things, what is it you have got,
Although we grant you get the thing you seek?

TOMMY ROBINSON
Marry, the removing of the illegals, who steal advantage of the poor citizens of this country.

SADIQ KHAN
Grant them removed, and grant that this your noise
Hath chid down all the majesty of England;
Imagine that you see the wretched strangers,
Their babies at their backs and their poor luggage,
Plodding to th' ports and costs for transportation,
And that you sit as kings in your desires,
Authority quite silent by your brawl,
All clothed with Stone Island and certainty;
What had you got? I'll tell you: you had taught

>How insolence and strong hand should prevail,
>How order should be quelled; and by this pattern
>Not one of you should live an aged man,
>For other ruffians, as their fancies wrought,
>With self same hand, self reasons, and self right,
>Would shark on you, and men like ravenous fishes
>Would feed on one another.

TOMMY ROBINSON
Bollocks.

THIRD RIOTER
By Arthur Watchins I told you he is a sound speaker: let's mark him.

SADIQ KHAN
>Let me set up before your thoughts, good friends,
>On supposition; which if you will mark,
>You shall perceive how horrible a shape
>Your riot bears: You'll put down these strangers,
>Beat them, black their eyes, possess their hotels.
>Say now the police should charge you for these crimes
>And then did banish you, whether would you go?
>What country, by the nature of your error,
>Should give you harbour? Go you to France or Flanders,
>To Iraq, Syria, Afghanistan?
>Nay, any where that not adheres to England,
>Why, you must needs be strangers: would you be pleased
>To find a nation of such barbarous temper,
>That, breaking out in hideous violence,
>Would not afford you an abode on earth,
>Whet their detested knives against your throats,
>Spurn you like dogs, and like as if that God
>Owed not nor made not you, nor that the claimants

Were not all appropriate to your comforts,
But chartered unto them, what would you think
To be thus used? This is the strangers' case;
And this your mountanish inhumanity.

FIRST RIOTER

Faith, a says true: let's do as we may be done to.

THIRD RIOTER

I yield, and desire Sadiq's mercy.

TOMMY ROBINSON

Hang on, I just seen a livestream on Facebook there's a nonce over there.

RIOTERS

Get him! *Exeunt separately.*

SCENE VII

CCHQ.

Enter a wet RISHI SUNAK, OLIVER DOWDEN, DAVID CAMERON, PENNY MORDAUNT, MICHAEL GOVE, KEMI BADENOCH, JEREMY HUNT, MICHELLE DONELAN, JAMES CLEVERLY *and Attendants.*

RISHI SUNAK

I know a bank where the wild slime flows,
Where Tampons and the bobbing floater goes,
Quite water-companied with fetid coastline,
With sweet discharges and pretexts asinine.
There shit the Tories some time of the night,
Poll'd in these faeces with dances and delight;
Where scorned Nadine scowls in her deep chagrin,

Pee deep enough to drown a Coffey in:
With its juice we'll streak th'electorates' eyes,
Fill voters full of hateful fantasies.
My plan is working, I've sought out the King.
The election's called, we're going to win!

OLIVER DOWDEN
And yet …
'Tis strange, these polls th'advisors speak of.

RISHI SUNAK
More strange than true. I never may believe
These sampling agents, and their fairy polls.

PENNY MORDAUNT
Polls! Advisors! Strange! You silly men.
What about London's mayoralty and our
Disastrous local election results?

MICHAEL GOVE
Oh Penny, people protest vote in these.
Our supporters are men with seething brains,
Such shaping fantasies, that apprehend
More than cool liberal ever comprehends.
The patriot, chauvinist, and the bigot
Are of whimsied fearfulness all compact:
And see more devils than vast hell can hold;
They, the frightened Home Counties, all as frantic,
See looming danger in a refugee:
The Tory's eye, in a fine frenzy rolling,
Doth glance from council house to council house
And as imagination bodies forth
The forms of felonies, their petty mind
Fates them as criminals, condemned for naught:
Homeless, disabled, kids on free school meals.

Such votes hath strong insecurity,
That if it would but apprehend some joy,
It comprehends some reason it were bad
And in the night, imagining some fear,
How easy is a bush supposed a boat?
Cruelty, for cruelty's sake, wins votes.

JAMES CLEVERLY
Yet in these stories told of illegals,
There grows to something of great constancy;
There's no smoke without fire, nor truth without ire.

KEMI BADENOCH
Tis true. Benefit cheats steal from us all.

RISHI SUNAK
Burdening my wife with millions in
Tax, cruelly forcing her to non-non dom.

JAMES CLEVERLY
Thus, when our chances face the slaughterhouse
It matters not if founded these fears are.

DAVID CAMERON
Here comes young Grant Shapps, full of joy and mirth.
Shappshifter, friends, who do you play this day?

Enter GRANT SHAPPS.

GRANT SHAPPS
Well, today, David, says my lanyard: 'Grant!'
News just in by the way, I've just heard that
A riot has just broken out at a
Refugee hotel. How on earth did our
Cynical choice not to process their claims,
But instead use our fellow humans as
Cheap political footballs with which to
Score endless own goals, mutate into a

Morally abhorrent catastrophe?
RISHI SUNAK
  The plan is working. What masq–
DAVID CAMERON
  Oh yes, what masques, what dances shall we have,
  To wear away this long age of three hours
  Before embarking on the battle bus.
  Where is our usual manager of mirth?
  What revels are in hand? Is there no play
  To ease the anguish of a pre-hustings hour?
  Call Jacob Rees-Mogg.   *Enter* JACOB REES-MOGG.
JACOB REES-MOGG
Here, Lord Cameron, and warm welcome back to our
  Maginot Line.
DAVID CAMERON
  Oh Mogg, you ghastly, self-fulfilling man.
  Say, what abridgment have you for this evening?
  What masque? What music? How'll we beguile the
  Calm before the door knocking storm?
JACOB REES-MOGG
Here's a brief how many sports are ripe, make choice which
  we'll see first.   *Giving a paper to* SUNAK.
DAVID CAMERON   *Taking the paper from* SUNAK, *reads:*
  'The Sinking of the *General Belgrano*,
  Sung a cappella, by one Laurence Fox.'
  We'll none that we hear Gino daily sing
  In glory of Maggie our kinswomen.
  'The riot of the tipsy Bullingdons,
  Tearing the Oxford bistro in their rage?'
  That is an old device, and it is play'd

Whenever our boys burn notes afore tramps.
'The Diary of a Secret Tory.'
That is some satire, keen and critical,
Not in the vein of our election mood.
'Mark Menzies using campaign money to
Get himself ransomed out of a flat.' No.
'The dance of the Home Office bullies.' No.
'Rob Jenrick's planning favours freestyle.' Nah.
'Neil Parish's sexy tractor porn strip.' No.
'A Chris Chope interpretive dance on why
He blocked the upskirting bill's progress.' No.
'Des Swayne blacking up's face for no reason.' No.
'The Owen Paterson Randox jive?' Nope.
'A Peter Bone genital ballet.' No.
'Lobbying at the trial of Elphicke and
Natalie's defection and denial
His wife and Hammer of the Trots.' No thanks.
'Matt Hancock rapping about snogging his
Aide Gina in store cupboards.' Lord spare us.
Good heavens, what is wrong with people who
Wish to represent Conservatives?
'A tedious brief scene from the Red Wall
Performèd by their boldest, finest minds.'
Tedious and brief? That is some hot ice.
What are they that do play it?

JACOB REES-MOGG

    Northerners, who've never inherited aught, and never labour'd
    In their minds till now; And now have toil'd their unbreathèd memories

With this strange party-political broadcast they have
   themselves made.
DAVID CAMERON
   And we will hear it.
JACOB REES-MOGG
   No, my noble lord, it is not for our kind: I have heard it over,
   They lack our, sharp, studied, cerebral, sesquipedalian
      drawl.
DAVID CAMERON
   We will hear that play;
   For never anything can be amiss
   When simpleness and racism tender it.
   Go, bring them in, Jacob.   *Exit* REES-MOGG.
PENNY MORDAUNT
   I love not to see wretchedness o'ercharged,
   And duty in his service perishing.
MICHAEL GOVE
   Why, Penny, you joined the wrong party then.
PENNY MORDAUNT
   Mogg says they can do nothing in this kind.
MICHAEL GOVE
   Mogg is a twat. Tis an open secret.
DAVID CAMERON
   The kinder we, Pen, to give thanks for naught.
   Our sport shall be then, to patronise our
   Red Wall pets. What they can't do, noble minds
   Takes it in might, not merit.
   Remember when shy Lee Anderson first
   In Commons spoke premeditated speech?
   And we did see him shiver and look pale,
   Make periods in the midst of sentences,

Throttle his practis'd accent in their fears,
And, in conclusion, dumbly did break off,
Not saying ought at all. And Penny, yet
Out of this silence yet we pick'd his thoughts;
And in the modesty of fearful duty
We read as much his racism
And saucy and audacious prejudice.
And therefore, with tongue-tied simplicity
The least speak most to my capacity.

Enter JACOB REES-MOGG.

JACOB REES-MOGG
So please it you my Lord David Cameron of Chipping Norton,   *SUNAK coughs.*
And the right honourable Rishi Sunak. The Prologue's address'd.

RISHI SUNAK
Let him then approach.

DAVID CAMERON
Let him then approach.

Flourish of trumpets. Enter the PROLOGUE.

MIRIAM CATES AS PROLOGUE
If we offend, it is with our good will.
That you should think, we do come to offend,
With pure ill will. To show our vicious skill,
That is the true beginning of our end.
Consider then, we come but in despite.
We do not come, as minding to content you,
Our true intent is. All for your delight
We are not here. That you should here repent you,
The Red Wall is at hand, and, by their show,
You shall know all that you are like to know.

DAVID CAMERON
This lady doth not stand upon points.
MICHAEL GOVE
She hath rid her prologue like a Tory in a brothel; she knows
   not the stop. A good moral, my lord: it is not enough to
   speak, but to speak true. Apart from in politics.
JEREMY HUNT
Indeed she hath played on this prologue like Gullis at
   PMQs; a sound, but not in government.
RISHI SUNAK
I agree, her speech was all disordered.
DAVID CAMERON
   We've just covered that, Rishi. Who is next?
      Enter JONATHAN GULLIS, BRENDAN CLARKE-SMITH, NICK
        FLETCHER, ANDREA JENKYNS *and* MARK JENKINSON.
MIRIAM CATES AS PROLOGUE
   Gentles, perchance you wonder at this show;
   But wonder on, till truth make all things plain.
   This man is Gullis, like you didn't know;
   This beauteous lady Jenkyns is certain.
   This man, with lime and rough-cast, doth present
   Wall, that Red Wall which does refugees sunder;
   And through Wall's chink, poor souls, they are content
   To whisper, at the which let no man wonder.
   This man, with lamp, taser and sniffer dog,
   Presenteth Border Force, for, if you know,
   By them do these refugees think no scorn
   To economically migrate here.
   This grisly beast (which Illegal by name)
   The trusty Jenkyns, coming first by night,
   Did scare away, or rather did affright;
   And as she fled, her Dryrobe she did fall;

Which Illegal, with bloody mouth did stain.
Anon comes young Gullis, sweet youth, and tall,
And finds his trusty Jenkyns' Dryrobe slain;
Whereat with flight, with forceful ferried flight,
He fearless fought the frightful foreign foe;
And Jenkyns, tarrying in hangar bright,
With paddles helped it taxi. The rest you know,
Let's strap the lot to Rwanda-bound plane,
And them deport with no leave to remain.
    Exeunt PROLOGUE, RED WALL, ILLEGAL, BORDER FORCE,
                                                         GULLIS *and* JENKYNS.

DAVID CAMERON
  I wonder if the Illegal be to speak.

JEREMY HUNT
  No wonder, ma'am. One Illegal may, when many asses do.

BRENDAN CLARKE-SMITH
  In this same interlude it doth befall
  That I, Clarke-Smith by name, present Red Wall:
  And such a Wall as I would have you think
  That wishes people in small boats would sink,
  The whole north, standing behind Union Jack,
  Did holler – that they want their country back.
  These vowels, this flat cap, and this pie doth show
  I speak for the north all. The truth is so:
  And this the cranny is, right and sinister,
  Through which the fearful migrants try to enter.

DAVID CAMERON
  Would you desire a Barratt new-build to speak better?

MICHAEL GOVE
  It is the wittiest partition that ever I heard discourse, my lord.

PENNY MORDAUNT
   Gullis draws near the Red Wall; silence.
                              Enter JONATHAN GULLIS.

JONATHAN GULLIS
   O grim-look'd Stoke! O Stoke with hue so black!
   O Stoke, which ever art when day is not!
   O Stoke, O Stoke, alack, alack, alack,
   I fear Potteries' promise is forgot!
   And thou, Red Wall, O sweet, O lovely wall,
   That stand'st between old Labour's ground and mine;
   Red Wall, Red Wall, O sweet and lovely wall,
   Show me thy chink, to blink through with mine eyne.
                              WALL holds up his fingers.
   Thanks, courteous wall: Gove shield thee well for this!
   But what see I? No Illegals do I see.
   O superb wall, through whom I see such bliss,
   Bless'd be thy stones for thus protecting me!

DAVID CAMERON
   The wall, methinks, being sensible, should thank him.

JONATHAN GULLIS
   No, in truth, sir, he should not. 'Protecting me' is
      Andrea's cue: she is to enter our party-political
      broadcast now, and I am to spy her through the wall.
      You shall see it will fall pat as I told you. Yonder she
      comes.
                              Enter ANDREA JENKYNS.

ANDREA JENKYNS
   Red Wall, full often hast thou heard our moans,
   'We're not deporting enough refugees.'
   For Southern MPs have oft lacked thy stones,
   Stones to expel unwanted emigrés.

JONATHAN GULLIS
  I see a voice; now will I to the chink,
  To spy an I can hear Andrea's face.
  Jenkyns?
ANDREA JENKYNS
  Gullis thou art, Gullis I think?
JONATHAN GULLIS
  MP for Stoke on Trent Kidsgrove and Talke;
  And, unlike Lee Anderson, trusty still.
ANDREA JENKYNS
  Traitorous defector, a grifting shill.
JONATHAN GULLIS
  Like Barry to Janine, I love our flag.
ANDREA JENKYNS
  As, Janine to Barry, I'm no Reform slag.
JONATHAN GULLIS
  Economic migrants, we must deport all.
ANDREA JENKYNS
  Send them to Rwanda, or England'l fall
JONATHAN GULLIS
  Wilt thou at Churchill's tomb meet me straightway?
ANDREA JENKYNS
  'Tide life, 'tide death, I come without delay.
BRENDAN CLARKE-SMITH
  Thus has Clarke-Smith, my part discharged so;
  And, being done, Red Wall away doth go.
            Exeunt CLARKE-SMITH, GULLIS *and* JENKYNS.
JEREMY HUNT
Now is the border down between the two neighbours.
MICHAEL GOVE
They'll put one in the Irish Sea next.

DAVID CAMERON
This is the wackiest stuff that ever I heard.
PENNY MORDAUNT
I cringe to share these benches with them.
MICHAEL GOVE
Unless imagination amend them, I doubt you'll have to for much longer.
PENNY MORDAUNT
Maybe I'll step down like everyone else.
RISHI SUNAK
We're off to LA.
DAVID CAMERON
Penny, calm down, dear. If we imagine no worse of them than they of themselves, they may pass for excellent politicians.
MICHAEL GOVE
Look. Here come two noble beasts in, a Border Force Agent and an Illegal.

Enter NICK FLETCHER as ILLEGAL and MARK JENKINSON as BORDER FORCE.

NICK FLETCHER
You, ladies, you, whose gentle hearts do fear
The smallest monstrous mouse that creeps on floor,
May now, perchance, both quake and tremble here,
When Illegal, on scary rampage roars.
Then know that I'm Nick Fletcher, macho man,
Not some Illegal on's benefit scam;
For if I as Illegal come in strife
Into this place, 'twere pity on my life.
PENNY MORDAUNT
A very gentle illegal immigrant, and of a good conscience.

KEMI BADENOCH
The very best at a bogus claimant that e'er I saw.
GRANT SHAPPS
  He speaks honestly, which rules him out of being a Tory.
MICHAEL GOVE
It sounds to me like he needs a strong positive male role model.
DAVID CAMERON
Nick, I heard 'the Equalizer' is being played by Queen Latifah now.   *FLETCHER squeals.*
MARK JENKINSON
  This lanthorn doth roaming search light present.
DAVID CAMERON
I'm surprised he could find a post-Brexit pumpkin to carve.
MICHAEL GOVE
Listen, Dave, we've all had enough of exports.
DAVID CAMERON
Bravo, Mike.
RISHI SUNAK
Isn't it experts?
MARK JENKINSON
  This lanthorn doth roaming search light present;
  Myself UK Border Force do seem to be.
JEREMY HUNT
This is the greatest error of all the rest; He wears no Serco high-vis.
MICHAEL GOVE
No Serco! Then who in government profited from the contract?
PENNY MORDAUNT
I am aweary of this agent. Would he would deport someone.

DAVID CAMERON
It appears by his small light of discretion that he probably isn't very good at it; but yet, in courtesy, in all reason, we must stay the time.

MICHAEL GOVE
Proceed, Agent.

MARK JENKINSON
All that I have to say, is to tell you that the lantern is a search light; I, a UK Border Force Agent; this taser my taser; and this dog my dog.

MICHAEL GOVE
Would the RNLI were equipped so. But silence; here comes Andrea Jenkyns. *Enter ANDREA JENKYNS.*

ANDREA JENKYNS
This is old Churchill's tomb. Where is my love?

NICK FLETCHER
Another woman! *ILLEGAL squeals again, JENKYNS runs off.*

MICHAEL GOVE
Well roared, Illegal.

DAVID CAMERON
Well run, Jenkyns.

PENNY MORDAUNT
Well shone, Border Force Agent.

FLETCHER tears JENKYNS' Dryrobe, and exits.

DAVID CAMERON
Well moused, Nick.

MICHAEL GOVE
And then came Gullis.

KEMI BADENOCH
Where has the Illegal gone? I know they're only acting, but it's best not to take chances. *Enter JONATHAN GULLIS.*

ACT V, SCENE VII | 225

JONATHAN GULLIS
　Search light, I thank thee for thy sunny beams;
　I thank thee, light, for shining now so bright;
　For, by thy gracious golden, glittering gleams,
　I trust to take of scary migrant's sight.
　But stay! O shite!
　But mark, search light,
　What dreadful dole is here!
　Eyes, do you see?
　How can it be?
　O Andrea! O dear!
　Thy Dryrobe good,
　What, stained with blood?
　Approach, ye no-go hell!
　O Fates, come, come;
　Blame foreign scum;
　Frame, crush, scapegoat, and quell!
DAVID CAMERON
This passion, and the loss of a lot of money on the stock
　market, would go near to make a man look sad.
PENNY MORDAUNT
　Beshrew my heart, but I pity this Gullis.
JONATHAN GULLIS
　O wherefore, Nature, didst thou migrants frame,
　Since migrants vile hath come to steal jobs thus?
　They, who then our benefits system game,
　Don't live, don't love, don't like, don't look like us.
　Come, jeers, confound!
　Out, knife, and wound
　These rafts RNLI;
　Ay, those woke saps,
　Their boats we'll pop:

Thus sink they: bye, bye, bye.
Now are they dead,
Now are they fled;
And Serco lights the sky.
Britannia, stand, fight!
Rwanda take flight!
Migrants bye, bye, bye, bye.

Exeunt GULLIS *and* JENKINSON.

DAVID CAMERON
Bye.

MICHAEL GOVE
Such useful idiots, who think spending six hundred thousand pounds per person to deport two hundred to Rwanda is a solution, rather than the manifest contempt of cruelty for cruelty's sake.

JEREMY HUNT
With the help of a brain surgeon they might acquire the power of critical thought.

DAVID CAMERON
A up. How chance Border Force is gone before Jenkyns comes back to wave off the deportation flight?

RISHI SUNAK
She will find him by gaslight.

PENNY MORDAUNT
She will find him by gaslight.

DAVID CAMERON
Oh bravo, Penny.

MICHAEL GOVE
Bravo!

RISHI SUNAK
I said that first.

DAVID CAMERON
Be quiet. *Enter ANDREA JENKYNS.*
JEREMY HUNT
Here she comes, and her passion ends the play.
PENNY MORDAUNT
I hope she will be brief.
MICHAEL GOVE
A mote will turn the balance, which Gullis, which Jenkyns, is the better: he for a man, God warrant us; she for a woman!
DAVID CAMERON
She hath spied him already with those hollow eyes.
ANDREA JENKYNS
  Oh hound of Stoke,
  Brave scourge of woke,
  Asylum seekers' block,
  The migrants' scourge
  Leads Islam's purge
  Not letting boats here dock.
  Chauvinist chimp,
  Resentful simp,
  Who blames lone stateless tots,
  Lee's gone, your up,
  Cheap, stand-in chump;
  Braying back bench blot.
  With bovine moos,
  Repeat your views,
  Denigrate refugees;
  Blame them for all,
  Shore up Red Wall
  Dispatch to Kigali.

Good, snub their plight:
Come, trusty flight,
Come, plane, migrants accrue;
And farewell, 'friends'.
Else Britain ends.
Adieu, adieu, adieu.

DAVID CAMERON
Border Force is left to sort out the eye-wateringly expensive deportation flights.

RISHI SUNAK
Ay, and Gullis too.

JONATHAN GULLIS
No, I assure you; Mark isn't actually in Border Force. It was a metaphor. Which is French for exaggerate. I only took on Deputy Chair at the last minute because Lee defected. Will it please you to see the epilogue, or to watch a patriotic Morris dance between some of our blacked-up company?

DAVID CAMERON
No epilogue, I pray you; for your party political broadcast needs no excuse. Never excuse; even when your output looks like a week two losing *Apprentice* challenge. For when election hopes are as dead as ours, there need none to be blamed. We'll just wash our hands, and move on to lecture circuits, or back to our Shepherd's Huts and Dubai-based consultancies; You won't. You'll return to your Red Wall shit holes. But the real Tories, the entitled elite, will. Don't look sad. Take heart. Your National Front message was truly and very notably discharged. And I'm sure it will connect well with the garden-centre bigots and lobotomised thugs where you come from. But come, your Bergomask; let your epilogue alone.

Music: Chas and Dave, 'Rabbit'. Here a dance of Clowns.
The iron tongue of midnight hath told twelve.
Tories, to bed; 'tis almost polling time.
I fear we all shall lose our seats this day.
As much as we have brought this on ourselves,
Our consciences will remain well beguil'd
By swelling bank accounts. Sweet friends, go to your
Publics, and there memento Tory
We're the ones born to rule, that's it. End of story.

Exeunt.

EPILOGUE

Enter CHORUS.

CHORUS
Thus far with rough and all-unable pen
Our bending author hath pursued the story,
In little room confining paltry men,
Mangling by starts the full course of their glory.
Small time, but in those fourteen years there lived
These Tsars of England. Fortune made their grifts,
By which the world's worst bequest they achieved
And left it to their bland impersonators,
Keir Starmer's Labour, who did the regime tail,
And by not being them, did seal the hollow crown,
A state so many had mismanagèd,
Lost to plutocrats, all assets sold,
Which oft our stage hath shown. And for their sake,
In your fair minds let this acceptance take.